BLOOD TRAIL

Undercover Series Book 3

Ruchi Singh

Copyright © Ruchi Singh 2022
All Rights Reserved.

ISBN 978-1-63669-572-3

This book has been published with all efforts taken to make the material error-free after the consent of the author. However, the author and the publisher do not assume and hereby disclaim any liability to any party for any loss, damage, or disruption caused by errors or omissions, whether such errors or omissions result from negligence, accident, or any other cause.

While every effort has been made to avoid any mistake or omission, this publication is being sold on the condition and understanding that neither the author nor the publishers or printers would be liable in any manner to any person by reason of any mistake or omission in this publication or for any action taken or omitted to be taken or advice rendered or accepted on the basis of this work. For any defect in printing or binding the publishers will be liable only to replace the defective copy by another copy of this work then available.

Blood Trail

Undercover Series

Book 3

By

Ruchi Singh

To
Varun

Books By Ruchi Singh

English

Novels

Romantic Suspense

The Bodyguard - Undercover Sries Book #1

Guardian Angel - Undercover Series Book #2

Blood Trail - Undercover Series Book #3

Everything Is Fair In Love

Romance

Jugnu - The Firefly

Take 2 - Small Town Girl #1

My Love, A Liar - Small Town Girl #2

Bewitched - Miracle Series Book #1

Cursed - Miracle Series Book #2 (Coming Soon)

Fiction Short Stories

Women From Mars : Series Shorts

Temptation

Spark

Romance Short Stories

You and Only You

Silent Love

A Promise is a Promise

Prologue

The doctor for the dead muttered a veiled curse for the caller after he switched off the phone. Pissed off by the fact that he had been woken up to do an autopsy so late at night. It had always been like that. "Buggers!" They had to do things in the pitch of darkness.

But then their profession demanded it, and the doctor was in no position to complain. He was paid handsomely for all the late-night troubles they would pile on him—so handsomely that his next seven generations could live a lavish life without earning a single dime.

In this scenario, who was he to complain?

Thankfully, the assistant was already at the morgue and had everything ready. Owing to the lateness of the hour and the fact that the doctor had had a drinking orgy with his friends late last night, he failed to notice the pale pallor and the red, puffy eyes of his assistant, who stood stoically beside the autopsy table, his eyes turned away from the corpse.

Taking a shallow breath, the doctor took his position at the cold table in the autopsy room. Details of the postmortem of unnatural deaths had to be recorded. He had been briefed about the case and knew the damage to the body. Conscious of the camera angles, he stood where the view of the patient's torso was blocked by his shoulders and began his examination.

Barely an hour later, he completed the report that presented his expert opinion.

'Cause of death: Hypovolemic shock, secondary to massive internal and external hemorrhage due to road traffic accident.

Gall bladder missing: Result of a previous cholecystectomy.'

His report failed to mention that both the kidneys of the dead man were missing too.

———◈◈◈———

Climbing up the winding staircase, he took off his diamond cufflinks and loosened his silk tie. The security light for the apartment on the top floor was green, which meant she was inside, keeping up her vigil.

He keyed in the password and the door opened with a faint click. Taking a deep breath, he entered the most private and precious part of his world. The plush carpet muffled his footsteps, thus not disturbing the two occupants of the room. He placed his cufflinks and tie on the credenza near the door and took off his jacket.

He studied his sleeping angels—one on the bed still under anesthesia, and the other on the easy, reclining sofa beside the bed. Though the pallor of the little one was a bit pale, his heartbeat was steady and regular on the monitors hooked around the bed.

Sensing her eyes on him, he smiled and moved toward her and lay down beside her taking her in his arms. She sighed, shifted, and snuggled against him, and he took strength from the fact that, for now, everything was under control.

Disaster had been averted. He closed his eyes and prayed for the long life of his loved ones.

———◈◈◈———

CHAPTER ONE

The blazing inferno didn't bother the tramp running out of the warehouse as the flames spread all around, engulfing the dilapidated area with unbridled gusto. The town clock chimed three times in the wee hours of the night.

He had, after all, taken the precaution of diving in the rusty water tank and wrapping a water-soaked blanket around himself, before he had lit the match and touched it to the ribbon of petrol that he had strategically spilled all over the floor of the warehouse.

Once out of the area and the danger, he shrugged off whatever was left of the smoking blanket and walked out of the slum where he had been living for the past many years. With unhurried steps, he walked through the narrow streets where people were beginning to wake up, sensing that there was something wrong in the vicinity.

Unnoticed due to the rising commotion, the tramp soon reached the main road, oblivious to a man following him. The man, in a pair of blue jeans and a grey T-shirt, which had clearly seen better days, followed the tramp, keeping a safe distance in between.

As the tramp reached a black car parked on the roadside, the man behind jogged closer, simultaneously, the rear door of the car opened. The man in the jeans threw a mask over the tramp, pushed him inside, and jumped in himself. The car began to move even before the rear door was pulled close. Speeding up, the car turned a sharp right, moving away from the hubbub of the town and the rushing fire engines on the opposite side of the road.

As the first ray of sunlight appeared on the horizon, the car steadily moved out of the city area and joined the highway, where it neared a container truck. A few minutes later, the rear-plank of the container slowly swung down from the top, forming a ramp in front of the car. The car accelerated and went up the ramp and inside. The door of the container closed without making a sound and the huge vehicle sped up in the direction of the national capital.

⸺⬦⬦⬦⬦⬦⸺

As the container truck headed to Delhi via the national highway, the passengers in the car inside came out one by one—the driver, the man in the jeans, and finally, the tramp.

"God! From where did you find this filthy rag, Karan? It's stinking!" The tramp threw off the mask and glared at the man in jeans.

"Welcome back, bro." Karan, the man in the grey T-shirt, hugged the tramp, sweaty clothes, dirty, matted hair and all. "You smell so good that I could kiss you!" Karan joked masking the worry that had refused to leave him when his brother, Armaan, had taken the undercover assignment two years ago. It was a relief that Chief had decided to bring him back, and he now stood safe and sound in front of him.

The driver of the car laughed. "Had heard somewhere that beggars can't be choosers."

"Good to see you too, Junaid. And I'm not a beggar. I'm a junkie drug dealer. Show some respect."

They all laughed, relieved and relaxed.

"Was this charade for extraction really necessary?" Armaan asked.

"Just to fool any eyewitnesses. It was Karan's idea." Junaid grinned.

"This or planting a body in your room. This seemed easier, cleaner, and untraceable."

Armaan nodded and sat down on a seat screwed to the wall of the container, lowering his guard for the first time in two years. Looking at him, no one could guess the turmoil brewing inside him, that need to stop the screams of the slum reverberating in his ears, that deep yearning to wipe off those horrific scenes, that drug users called life, from his mind. But it was curtains on the oath he had taken on the pyres of his parents years ago.

"Got you some clean clothes and a shaving kit." Karan held out a bag, bringing Armaan out of his reminiscences. "Spare us the torture and dump the trash you have been wearing, since I don't know how many months, in this drum." He banged an empty metal drum, about three feet in height, kept in the corner. "I have a matchbox. The fire will kill the crawling and breeding germs, as we have just witnessed."

"He'll need gardening scissors to hack through that jungle on his face." Junaid took a seat on the L-shaped wooden bench that was screwed onto one of the corners of the container and took out a communication device, a laptop, and a Wi-Fi dongle connecting to the headquarters on an unknown frequency.

"It's all in there, the scissors, a trimmer, soap, a towel, and even an antiseptic lotion," Karan said wetting a washcloth from a bottle and handing it to Armaan. "This should be enough for the time being. The rest of the cleaning will happen after we've reached home."

Wrapping a towel around himself, Armaan stripped and dumped his clothes in the metal drum. He hacked on his two-year-old beard and even cut some of his hair that was spilling over his shoulders. He began to feel half-human again as he pulled on clean underwear, jeans, and a black T-shirt, after washing his face and sponging off his body with the washcloth.

He cleaned himself as much as he could given the circumstances, as he heard the update on Junaid's wireless device about the various godowns and offices of North India's biggest drug mafia being raided. Copious amounts of illegal pharmaceutical drugs, as well as those on the streets being seized simultaneously.

"God! I feel so much better," he said after drinking half a bottle of water that Karan had handed him. "Do you have something to eat?"

"You bet." Karan handed him a take-out brown paper bag, which contained a cold sandwich and an apple.

"So?" Armaan asked with a mouthful, "Any specifics, Junaid."

"They are making arrests all over DK's offices and warehouses as we speak. You'll be able to observe the suspects' interview most probably by tomorrow," Junaid said looking at the laptop screen, "DK is on the run."

"He will lawyer up." Armaan sighed. "Though his accounts may have been frozen, he has friends in high places."

"Of course, he will, but he will be watched and be out of circulation," Karan consoled. "But we won't get Danish."

"No, we won't. All evidence against him is circumstantial. I've dogged him for every moment of the last six months, but couldn't find a single piece of solid evidence that can nail him. Do you have any news about the one named Nayak?"

"No." Junaid scowled. "But, I don't have all the updates as yet."

"He is the key, Junaid. He is the key."

⸺⸺

PRESENT DAY 0
GURUGRAM. NCR

The insistent shrill of the phone ringing disturbed Digvijay Kumar Huda, in his penthouse situated in a posh township in Gurugram. He muttered something inaudible, fondling his mistress' breasts, who didn't even stir. The phone stopped ringing and immediately sleep, like his mistress, pulled him back into its blissful clutches.

The moment he had settled, the phone rang again.

This time, the woman pushed his hand away and shifted to the other side of the bed. Losing the warmth of the soft body, the ringing irritated him even more. Muttering a curse, he stirred and glanced at the number flashing on the screen. All remnants of sleep left him in a microsecond. He threw the comforter off his body and sat up with a jerk. Out of the three phones and five SIMs that he owned, this one wasn't supposed to ring at all.

It meant only one thing.

Disaster had struck.

He picked up the phone. "DK."

"NCB raids at all the godowns. Police all over, everywhere. Leave now." The call was disconnected.

There was no time for questions and explanations. They were not required. It was time for action. He ran naked to the double door closet and pulled out a duffel bag.

"What happened, darling?" The woman raised her head and blinked.

"You have to leave." He pulled on his underwear before extracting a wad of notes from the bag and throwing them at the woman, who caught it expertly.

Her eyes went huge looking at the bonanza. Diwali had come early for her "When will we meet again?"

"Go to the other house. You have two minutes," he growled and slipped a T-shirt over his head.

The woman understood the panic and haste. Some of his fear rubbed on to her too and she scrambled out of the bed. Hurriedly donning her clothes and heels, she tried to make a list of what she should take and what she should leave.

"And Sonya, don't talk to anyone about anything. I'll pull out your nails one by one if you rat out to anyone. I'll know if you do." Now the fear was palpable, as she raked her brains to gather her things which may or may not link her to this hateful man. Not that she knew anything, but now she would try to forget even the tidbits that had fallen into her ears.

DK packed his bag, picked up his laptop and three phones, and left the apartment.

The drive to the safe house was completed in silence. The 'hows' and 'whys' of the catastrophe would have to wait. The need was to not get into the authorities' hands before the clean-up.

DK's phone pinged again, but he ignored it as he drove slightly under the city speed limit. Drawing unnecessary attention of the traffic police would be foolish under the circumstances. Even then, he reached the safe house in record time, primarily due to the early hour of the day. A faint line of the moon could still be seen on the horizon when he pulled into the driveway of the property at the outskirts of Gurugram.

The farmhouse, under his close friend's dead mother's name, had a cozy little two-story bungalow, with a sprawling farm all around, a hidden basement, and a tunnel underneath, which could be used in case he was ambushed here. There was skeletal staff for the upkeep—just one housekeeper and a guard at the gate. He had pinged his loyal bodyguard, Jadhav, and he too would be arriving after collecting more information from his source in the police department.

Barking instructions to the guard at the gate to close down and to only let Jadhav in, he went to his office in the basement, locked the door, and switched on the computer. He knew by heart the login details of the app he had to use in case of such an emergency. It was an obscure app that Nayak had commissioned right at the start of the business. An app used by only their organization. Its features were basic, except the security that was state of the art. It was the best way to communicate without getting caught.

There was no response from the other side.

⊶⊰⊹◈⊹⊱⊷

PRESENT DAY 0
LUTYENS, NEW DELHI

Trisha admired the imposing three-story bungalow situated in one of Delhi's poshest areas, Lutyens, as the guard waved her inside the ornate gates. She drove at a steady pace on the paved driveway and wondered whether she was a step closer to her mission or was getting entrenched into a dangerous quagmire of deceit and artifice.

The valet at the portico stood beside her car, politely waiting for her to alight and hand over the car keys. Taking a deep breath, she picked up the bouquet of lilies that had cost her quite a fortune and stepped out. The four steps up to the marble foyer led to a wide lobby and to the living room to her left, where she could hear the clink of glasses and live music.

She stood at the threshold of the large, carpeted living room and scanned the occupants. Clad in a beautiful aqua blue silk lounge dress which clung to her voluptuous figure appreciatively, her boss and host, Dr. Priya, stood talking to the Nephrology department's head at Zenith Hospitals. Her twin, Dr. Udit, who looked equally dashing in smart casuals, was at the bar mixing drinks for everyone. Quite a few years older than Trisha, he was a handsome man, with a confident air about him that came with money and all kinds of worldly experiences.

The siblings were Page 3 darlings. While the media extolled Priya's charity work, Udit kept them occupied with his romantic escapades all the year round. More so, because of their close relation to the royal Gaekwad family of a princely state in Gujrat.

Udit glanced at Priya, who too looked at him at the same time, and moved to another guest who stood alone and seemed a bit pensive. Their familiarity with each other, and their uncanny ability to understand each other without exchanging words was impressive; maybe it had something to do with them sharing a womb.

Apart from all the extracurricular activities and their celebrity status, the twins—Uditraj Gaekwad and Priyadarshini Gaekwad—were phenomenally intelligent and gifted surgeons, trained under their mother, Dr. Aishwarya Gaekwad, who had been a legend in the medical fraternity. She had expanded the Zenith chain of hospitals after inheriting the main hospital in Delhi from her father. The twins had inherited the hospital chain after she had passed away years back due to a sudden cardiac arrest. Her untimely demise was a shock to all who knew her.

However, even though the twins had to take over the responsibility of such a huge conglomerate at such short notice, they were doing phenomenally well, taking the chain to a height where it was touted as the best medical facility in South Asia.

The live band struck another song bringing her back to the present. She mentally shook her head and concentrated on the other guests in the room.

Surprised to find quite a few guests from the hospital, and the fact that she got the dress code right for the evening dinner, Trisha's heartbeat steadied a bit. Feeling confident in her deep green, mid-thigh dress with a scooped neck, she stepped forward into the swanky, modern room and smiled when Priya spotted her.

"Trisha, so happy that you could make it. You look lovely!"

"Thanks, Ma'am. You are too kind." She handed the bouquet to her.

"Are these for me! Thanks so much. They are lovely. Come and meet everyone." She pulled her into the room introducing her to a pretty brunette in a red gown and another lady in an eclectic, rainbow color gypsy dress.

Half an hour later, Trisha was bored. She had nothing in common with her hosts and the rest of their guests. Everyone was rich beyond her imagination and each one endlessly discussed the last foreign holiday they took or the amount they donated for charity or the nation's politics. Holding the cocktail glass in her hand, she moved out of the French doors to the side gardens, where a live band played soothing instrumental music.

"Would you like to dance?"

Trisha turned her head to see Udit stretching out a hand toward her. She looked around the beautiful blooming garden where no one else was dancing.

"Someone has to start, isn't it?" He smiled and answered her unspoken question.

She placed her hand in his, and he pulled her into a close yet impersonal grip. A few seconds later, two more couples joined them.

"So, what do you do in your free time, Trisha?" he asked, then chuckled softly. "Provided the hospital allows you the free time."

She smiled. "Nothing much. I read a bit."

"What kind?"

"Thrillers."

"Is it? Wow. That's interesting."

It seemed he didn't read because he didn't carry the conversation further. She didn't ask because she didn't want to embarrass him if he didn't. She had to be on good terms with them.

"Er… Trisha, would you like to come to the CJI's daughter's wedding reception with me?" he said after a while.

Oh! Trisha couldn't mask the surprise rolling on her face at the invitation. Udit was having a blazing affair with a nurse at the hospital. Everyone knew. Trisha had once seen them in a compromising position, and had withdrawn from the room before they could spot her.

"If you are busy, I completely understand that."

"No. It's just that my brother is a special needs child. If I can arrange for a babysitter, I'd love to come."

"Wonderful."

"I'll let you know in two days' time, if that's okay?" The music came to a stop.

"Yes, of course." He left her immediately and his hands went into the pockets of his trousers. "Thanks for the dance."

"My pleasure," Trisha said, hiding the insincerity from her tone. If she wasn't aware of his reputation, she would have thought he was shy around her.

"Shall I get you a refill?"

"No, no, I'm good, please carry on."

He bowed and went inside to tend to his other guests. Trisha interacted with a few people then wandered around the premises. She eyed the stairs in the lobby that led to the upper floor of the bungalow. Looking around at the living room, she quietly went up the stairs.

The first floor held a family living area and three doors, all of which were surprisingly locked. Trisha turned to the stairs to explore the second floor.

"Dr. Mehra!"

Trisha whirled around and got the shock of her life. What was the dragon doing here? Was she too invited to the party?

"What are you doing here?" The old woman scowled.

"Er… I was looking for the washroom, Ms. Paul." Trisha blinked her eyes and pointed to her purse. Changing tampons was the best excuse at times like this.

"It's downstairs. Really, Dr. Mehra, you should have asked one of the staff."

"Yeah, well, everyone looked awfully busy. I thought I shouldn't disturb anyone." She turned toward the stairs going down. "Er… you arrived late to the party, Ms. Paul?"

"No. I come here when Dr. Priya or Dr. Udit need any help. Though, I think that's none of your business."

Anger swirled at the tone. "Careful, Ms. Paul. I am one of the doctors on Zenith's panel, not a staff reporting to you. There's no need for you to be rude."

Ms. Paul pursed her lips and stood crossing her arms. Trisha matched her stony stare for a few seconds then marched down the stairs.

By the time she reached home late at night, her head was pounding with all the formality and constantly being on guard. But the visit was not wasted. She got the invitation to the most coveted party in the town. She knew they kept rooms locked. And she hoped she would get invited again.

⟨•⟩⟨◆⟩⟨•⟩

Do I really need to do this, Priya?" Udit asked as they unwound in their first-floor living room after the party.

"Yes," she said, though her heart protested at the idea vehemently.

"I don't want to be with any of those women. I'm fed up of dating and courting other women just to appease society." Udit poured a whiskey in a glass and drank it neat. "Worms crawl up my skin when I touch them."

"That's why you should marry. Then you'll have to tolerate only one woman."

"Still, is this the only solution?" He sounded like a sulky child and hated it. Priya was younger to him by two minutes but had him wound around her finger like no one. He could never refuse her anything.

"Yes. We have to keep up the pretense and be discreet, darling. Society will not be kind to us if they come to know. Our reputation, honor, our social standing—everything is at stake here."

"If I marry then I'll have to live somewhere else! I can't just leave you here with all the responsibilities." He sat down and caught hold of her hand. "I can't do that, Priya, you know that."

"You can always visit and we'll meet at the hospital. Most of the things are being managed from there. Moreover, I'll call you when I need you, so stay close by. I have even earmarked a property just half a kilometer from here. People have begun to talk, Udit, why both of us are single. And you know I can't marry. I can't let anyone into my life, or leave this house. We have to give them something else to discuss. This is the only way to keep tongues from wagging."

He stood up again. "Why us?"

"We are royalty, Udit. No matter how many generations pass, we'll always be royalty." Her face lit up like a queen's and her head tilted at an angle as if she was seated on a throne. "Isn't it so exciting? People look up to us like we are superior beings. We have to maintain that persona, our dignity, live up to the expectations. Did you ask Trisha to accompany you to the reception?" She changed the subject as Udit continued to stare at his glass.

"Yes. And you should have seen her expression when I asked, as if I had gone nuts."

"What did she say?"

"She'd let me know in a few days. The cold, calm speculation in her eyes irritates me. It's not respect that I see on her face, just resigned compliance because she wants to be in our good books."

"Then perhaps she is the right candidate for us. She'll always be with us because it seems, money is important to her. You know she has bought quite an expensive car. We have to keep her close, you know two birds, one stone and all that. And you can always visit here without any eyebrows being raised." She continued, when he shook his head, "Don't you see the power we wield? People are afraid of us. She would be under your thumb all her life. I think she will be the perfect candidate."

⸺◦⫷◈⫸◦⸺

PRESENT DAY 0. EVENING
NOIDA. NCR

After a short preliminary briefing to KN Rao, their boss and the director, of the Intelligence Bureau, at the IB headquarters, Armaan and Karan reached Karan's home in Delhi later that night.

"So?" Karan asked, putting the house and car keys in the bowl on the kitchen counter.

Armaan smiled. "Come here." He opened his arms and Karan stepped into his hug, burying his face in Armaan's shoulder. "I missed you, Ricky." A little overwhelmed Armaan enveloped his brother in a bone-crushing embrace.

"Missed you too, *bhai*." Karan didn't leave Armaan even when the latter loosened his hold.

The brothers had a family legacy of being in law enforcement. Their grandfather and father were in the army. Years ago, when their parents were brutally killed in an ambush by a group of hardcore druggies for just a small amount of money and their vehicle, both, Armaan and Karan, had sworn to bring down the entire drug mafia, which was funded by enemies of the nation across the border.

Armaan had been shocked by the senseless brutality to his parents but had kept a strong facade for Karan, who was just coming out of his teens when the tragedy struck them. And perhaps Karan thought the same and hid his anguish well by putting up a nonchalant, devil-may-care attitude.

"Hey." Armaan smiled, rubbing his back. "What happened? Are you wiping snot and what not on my shirt?"

"And what not." Karan sniffled and lifted his head. "It's great to have you back. This time, you took it too far."

"The information I was getting was too good to leave it midway."

"Yeah." He pinched his nose, a bit embarrassed at not being able to control his emotions. "Anyway, let's get drunk like old times."

"Like old times, yes. But you drink, I have to detox myself. Have been abusing my body for too long."

"As I said, you took it too far this time but not anymore."

"No, not anymore."

CHAPTER TWO

"Tushar, come out. Now!" With quick fingers, Trisha clipped the sides of the tiffin close and dropped it in the red backpack. "Tushar, we are getting late, sweetheart!" She checked her purse for her stethoscope and doctor's coat.

"I told you not to call me sweetheart." He appeared in the doorway, pouting, just as she had predicted. "I'm not a baby."

"Then stop acting like one, please." She stuffed the water bottle in the side slot of his backpack. "You are taking the bus to school today. I don't have time to drop you, Tush. Surgeries have to start at 8:00, or they will chuck me out."

She took another look at her brother, on his way to getting taller than her, sulking at the threshold of his room twisting the tie of his uniform and ruining the knot. An almost adult trapped in the mind of a seven-year-old, he stood with his head down, staring at his shoes. He had a test today and he totally detested geography. Her heart melted. "We'll have pizza for dinner."

His head shot up and a grin appeared on his grim face. "Even if I get a zero?"

She tried not to smile at the glee. "Even if you get a minus 10. But you have to do your best. Deal?"

"Deal!" He picked up his bag and rushed to the entrance where Kishore Dada, their long-time family friend, who helped her look after Tushar, waited to take him to the bus stop.

Trisha let out a deep breath and tidied the kitchen, before getting ready herself. The battle at home was won and now she had to move onto the second battle of her day—the hospital.

This week, she was determined to find out what the deal was with the topmost floor of the hospital, which remained locked for everyone except Dr. Udit, Dr. Priya, and the dragon.

***

DAY 1. MORNING
POLICE STATION. NEW DELHI

Armaan stood in the observation room of the Central Police Station in Delhi with Rao, monitoring the progress of the arrests and raids, and reading all the reports that the Narcotics Bureau and local police were filing in. The members of the gang were being brought in the holding room, attached to the observation room that had a two-way mirror window, so that Armaan could recognize the men he had come across during his undercover stint.

"Have they found a connection to Nayak? Any person or document?" Armaan asked.

"So far, no," Sharma, the man heading the police's Cyber Crime department and in-charge of all the documentary and electronics connections between the various business entities belonging to DK, answered.

"What about Danish?"

"DK and Danish cannot be traced at the moment. Though there is nothing in Danish's name, no connection with the business."

Armaan looked at the suspects from behind the two-way mirror and didn't feel the zing of success. "Something's missing. This is not it."

"How can you say that? We have the warehouse, the transit manifest, the money trail, the witnesses…well the whole package. And we also have their stash of fake passports from Pakistan, Iran, Afghanistan. Everything is right here. What more could be there?" Sharma glanced at Rao.

"I just keep getting this feeling…" Armaan raked his hair with his fingers. "With every passing second, I'm getting convinced that we don't have the entire pie. It's too smooth. It's a piece, but it's not the whole thing. What do we know about Nayak?"

"Nothing to add to what you have given us. DK is absconding with some of his faithfuls. We will apprehend him no matter what."

"DK is not the brain behind all this. He is just the operations guy. Nayak is the one." Armaan now paced the observation room.

"Okay, just relax," Rao finally said.

"I should have stayed on. I should've—"

"We have caught someone from one of the DK's bungalows on the outskirts of Amritsar. According to the driving license found on him, his name is Nayak Thande." Karan entered waving a paper. "They are booking and bringing him in."

"What?!" Armaan glanced at Rao then took the printout that had the data on the arrest.

"Okay, so DK has gone under and a person has been arrested who says his name is Nayak." Sharma too read the report.

"Can it be so easy?" Armaan scowled.

"Sometimes… it is easy," Rao said, looking at the next lot of suspects being logged in into the interview room. "I think you are thinking too much."

"He is the one," Karan said pointing toward the man in the interview room beyond, "the one with the tie."

Armaan stared at the tall, lanky man, wearing a crisp, pin-striped suit and a silver tie, glaring at the policemen and demanding to call his lawyers. The man didn't fit the image of the gang leader that was formed in Armaan's mind based on the stories he had heard when he was living with the gang for all those months.

"No, I don't think so…" Armaan shook his head. "No, he is not Nayak. He cannot be. You don't understand. Nayak is like God to them. He is revered in the organization. They are shit scared of just the name. You all don't understand…" Armaan waved his hand at the suspects around the man. "Look at them. Look into their eyes. They are sitting with him as if he is just one of them. There was palpable awe when they took his name back there. An aura… But here… Here, they are sitting as if he is one of them."

"I hear you, Armaan." Rao nodded and turned to his men. "So, team, let's go by what Armaan says. We will continue to look for DK and extradite him from whichever country or hole he has gone into. The same goes for Nayak as well, though he remains, at large, an unknown, unidentified entity, his file will remain open."

"I should've stayed in that place for one more year," Armaan muttered.

"The operation was getting riskier every day, not to mention its impact on your health," Rao said, looking at Armaan who had lost lots of weight, a result of the lack of nutrition during the undercover assignment. Given his role, Rao was sure he had to sample the illegals too to convincingly fraternize with the enemy.

"I could have sustained."

"No. We have enough proof to break the spine of their drug cartel. It is not going to be difficult to prove the surplus legal drugs being manufactured without approvals, as well as the illegal ones. Now that we have the root, we'll capture the branches too. What we have is enough."

Armaan stood silent watching the proceedings.

"And for Nayak, we'll lay down a new trap. We'll build on the leads you have and assign a separate team to take it up."

⋘⋄⋙

DAY 1, MORNING
ZENITH HOSPITAL, NEW DELHI

The dragon stared at Trisha from above her horn-rimmed spectacles as Trisha came out of the OT to the cleaning station.

"Dr. Mehra, a package has come for you. I have kept it in front of your locker in the residents' room."

"Thank you, Ms. Paul." Trisha took off her gloves and threw them into the dustbin.

"You need to confirm the party invite with Dr. Udit for the CJI's daughter's wedding."

Trisha tried not to grimace and continued washing her hands, her eyes on the faucet. She had raked her brains but she still couldn't fathom why he had extended the invitation to her. In all her time as a senior resident at the hospital and in the time she had known the Gaekwad family when her father was employed at the hospital, he had never shown any interest in her—personal or professional. All her dealings were with his sister.

Ms. Paul let out a phony cough prodding Trisha to answer.

Trisha didn't want to go, but this was the only way to get into the inner coterie of the Gaekwads. The question was not what she wanted but what she needed to do. And she had to get close to the Gaekwads—even if Udit was nine years her senior, even if Priya was a rich snob, and even if Trisha's suspicions about—

The coughing was louder the second time.

"I'd love to go." She smiled and turned toward Ms. Paul. "I'll inform Dr. Udit right away."

The dragon nodded with her lips pursed, though the froth Trisha imagined coming out of her nostrils had lost its bite. Trisha updated the patient's report then walked to the top floor where the Gaekwad siblings had their offices.

As she stepped onto the landing of the hallowed floor, the air changed. The lavish interiors, the reverent hush, and breathing silence raised the hair on the nape of her neck. It didn't look like a hospital but like a five-star hotel, even though she knew surgeries happened here. She had seen Ms. Paul wheeling a medicine trolley into the elevators to this floor. It had always been like that since the two months she had been allowed on this floor. This was the floor where sometimes Dr. Priya chose to spend the night too.

While sister and brother had the family bungalow, Dr. Priya had a small apartment on this floor as well. The reason cited was that she had work that often entailed her to spend late evenings in the hospital and she was too tired to go back home. Dragon too had a studio apartment on the same floor.

From the lift lobby, through the glass partition that led into the wide waiting room on the floor, she could see Dr. Priya standing near the window talking over the phone. She normally spoke softly, as if the conversation was a burden. Today, she did not have surgeries scheduled, so she was dressed in an ivory silk saree with thin, golden zari threads woven in random patterns. Her thick, straight hair spread over her shoulders touched her waist, while diamonds adorned her earlobes and fingers. She was indeed a beautiful woman.

As Trisha opened the door to the waiting room, she glanced toward the west wing and studied the wide doors painted in green and white floral pattern, doors that were always locked. This was where Trisha knew the answers to all her questions were.

She had to somehow find the means to open those doors. They were hiding something in there and she had to find it. She had taken a vow five years ago and all the clues that she had painfully followed had led her to this floor of the hospital. It would take some more time but she would find the key or a way to enter the west wing.

Dr. Priya'a interest in her gave her some undue advantages and access to various things happening in the hospital, but this floor was still off limits to her. One day… one fine day… Priya moved back to her office without spotting her.

Taking a deep breath, Trisha stepped forward and opened the door to Udit's office. "Hi."

Handsome as ever, he looked up and plastered a smile on his face. "Hey, Trisha."

She had a sense since the party that he tolerated her because of his sister.

"Did you need anything?" Udit asked politely.

"Er… I would love to go to the wedding reception… with you."

"Perfect, I'll pick you up—"

"No, no. I'll meet you in the lobby of the venue, if that's okay."

"Yes, of course. Works fine. Will reach there by seven. Ping me the moment you enter the gates of the hotel," he replied, hiding his exasperation well, but not too well.

"Sure." Trisha threw a shy smile and pulled the door shut. She turned and found herself face-to-face with Dr. Priya. "Hi, Ma'am."

"Hi, Trisha. I wanted to talk to you about the patient who had come for an appendectomy. I heard you forced the admin to give him a discount and then paid the balance out of your own pocket."

"Yes, Ma'am."

"Why? You know we are strictly against any discounts."

"Ma'am, he is a very poor man and his son needed that operation. The son is the sole earner. I know him."

"Then he should have gone to a government hospital. We are not running a charity organization, Trisha. These street people can't keep their fly zipped, breed like rodents, then expect us to shoulder their burdens. They are like parasites and should be avoided. I better not hear any such case again."

"Yes, Ma'am." Trisha looked down to hide the anger and disappointment bubbling inside.

"So, are you going with Udit?"

"Yes, Ma'am." She took a discreet breath again, looked up and smiled.

"I hope you have something nice to wear. Actually, why don't you come by in the evening and look at the dresses and saris I have?"

"No, no… Ma'am. I have an outfit for the occasion." Though seething at the insult, Trisha kept her mask of politeness in place. "In any case, I don't think I could carry or do justice to your ensemble."

Dr. Priya smiled condescendingly, nodded, then turned toward her offices, dismissing Trisha like someone beneath her station, she did not want to waste more of her time on.

Her polite and subservient expression in place, Trisha turned toward the elevators and went down to the residents' room. No matter what she did, she was unable to find a key to those rooms, nor had she seen anyone else going in or opening those doors. Her next hope was now her graveyard shift on Friday.

⚊⚊⚊•≼◈◈≽•⚊⚊⚊

DAY 1, EVENING
GURUGRAM, NCR

DK paced his small yet elegant office, huffing and seething. One of the most lucrative arms of his business had been wiped off. His investment in the facility in Punjab had just begun to return profits. But everything was gone in seconds! The police was swarming all around, poking at his personal effects in his offices and homes.

Their indigenous app pinged. DK tensed for a second then relaxed to see Jadhav's name on the screen. He swiped to take the video call. "How did it happen?"

"Someone knew everything about the operations. The revenue reports, transport manifests including the time, place, and the names of our men are with the police. They've frozen all the bank accounts too. There's been an information leak."

"Who did it?" DK lashed out.

"I need time—"

The pulse ticking on the jaw accelerated. "You find those answers for me, Jhadav, or I will shoot everyone down myself. And where is Danish?"

His bodyguard squirmed on the screen, hesitating.

"What?"

"Sir, no one has been able to connect with Danish for the past ten hours. He is not responding to our calls."

DK loosened his tie and shrugged out of his blazer, muttering something under his breath. "Okay, fine. You find the informant."

After his security head disconnected, DK went to the bar and poured himself two fingers of scotch and gulped it straight down. The news coming from the various offices was enough to mentally break anyone with a lesser spine, but he was made of sterner stuff. It was a massive financial loss, but he would recover for sure.

Moreover, it was a relief that he had kept the other business completely separate from this one, buried under layers of fictitious companies and the Board of Directors. So much so that even Danish, his half-brother, didn't have a clue.

The app pinged again and this time he mopped his brow with his fine linen handkerchief, then swiped to take the audio call.

"Have they connected the other business with this?" The caller asked without any preamble when they connected.

"No."

"Good. Keep it that way, or all will go down in no time."

"I intend to. Don't worry." He let out a sigh of relief, then got another jolt.

"DK, there was a leak from your end in Amritsar."

"What! No…I…let me—"

"No need. The deed is done. Someone from the IB infiltrated your gang, DK."

"The IB?"

"Yes."

"How did the IB get involved?"

"Apparently it started with our operations across the border."

"Fuck! We need to find that agent and tear him limb to limb!"

"No! You will do nothing of the kind."

"But he has to be punished…"

"No. The person who brought him in has to be punished. You know the IB. If you take revenge from one of them, the whole group will be after you and there is no stopping then."

"But—"

"I'm sending you the name of the agent and his alias. Find out who brought him in and fix the leak, then go underground as planned. I'll contact you when needed."

"How do you know about the agent and his alias?"

"Don't ask too many questions, DK, when I am trying to help you. Don't you know our reach?"

An image appeared on his screen. The caption on the image read: 'Major Armaan Joshi'

"Fuck!" DK hissed and took a screenshot.

CHAPTER THREE

So you are going with that dud?" Mahi asked, her voice muffled as she had her head and hands into Trisha's wardrobe looking for a perfect dress for the party.

After completing her DM, Trisha had been able to afford the two-bedroom apartment, so that Tushar and she could have separate bedrooms and in a better locality. Mahi, her neighbor had been godsend support and now was a constant in their lives—with Mahi babysitting Tushar, when Trisha had an emergency and Trisha accompanying Mahi on her morning power-walks, to help her lose postpartum weight.

"He is not a dud. Mahi. All the women in the hospital swoon over him—both the staff and the patients. And even their relatives. Everyone regardless of the sex."

"Well, if he doesn't swoon over you then for me he is a dud. Okay. maybe a handsome dud." She rolled her eyes and grinned.

Trisha laughed out loud. "Oh, Mahi, I love you. What would I do without you?"

"I love you too," Mahi said sifting through the dresses strewn on the bed, then sighed. "At least you are going out, that's a relief."

"What do you mean, at least?!" Trisha knew it was hopeless. She had nothing suitable to wear for a wedding reception.

"I don't remember the last time you had asked my help to dress up for a party. You never have fun." Mahi lifted her forefinger as soon as Trisha opened her mouth. "Dinner with Tushar doesn't count. Outing with a kid doesn't count, Trish. I meant you should have some unadulterated fun with someone your age. Tell me the last time you took a day off or went out for dinner."

"Umm…" Not meeting her eyes, Trisha tried to recall. "… Er…" She looked at the walls, then the ceiling. "Er…"

"Exactly!" Mahi clicked her fingers after a few seconds and glared at her. "Case closed. No argument. It's the Oberois for God's sake! You are going to have fun, regardless of your escort, who is…"

"Shush, Mahi. No one has any proof. Moreover, he is doing a nurse."

"So what?! Who said people can't do both? By the way, did you really see him holding her boob that day?"

"Mahi! I did not see his hand on her boob. He just went past her and his elbow brushed against her chest. It could be accidental."

"Whatever. It's still the same thing. Yucky! Ugh…" She then pulled out a black Chantilly lace dress from the pile on the bed. "This is it! This will look great on you. And I have just the right accessories to go with this one."

"A dress? It's a wedding reception!"

"I don't care. You are going to wear this and attract the right kind of attention and maybe get laid."

"God, Mahi! Keep your voice down."

"Trisha, you are twenty-nine and I am twenty-six and I get laid every day." She put her palm up. "Okay, maybe that's an exaggeration with Riya around, but I do get laid every other day. It's fun and relaxing."

"Easy for you to say that with a husband so handsome, who sleeps on the same bed." Mahi was married to her childhood sweetheart, Nikhil, and they had a cute little daughter, five-month-old Riya.

"That's what I am saying. You should get married too or at least have a relationship. It's high time."

"Don't you think it's a bit revealing? My cleavage will show." Trisha pulled up the black lace dress to her shoulders and looked into the mirror.

"Now, you are changing the subject. But it's okay, at least keep your mind open if you like someone. And yes, you will look smashing in it. That neckline is fine, not deep at all. There'll be plenty of other girls who will show so much that you will look like a matron. But this is perfect for you." Mahi jumped up from the bed. "I'll bring my earrings and the bracelet, and you can wear those copper-colored heels that you had bought last Diwali." Saying so she ran out to her apartment.

Trisha glanced at her reflection again. Mahi was not wrong, Trisha hadn't had a life after her father died. A batch mate and she were a couple during the third year of her MBBS, but that fizzled out when her father passed away and she ended up taking care of Tushar along with her studies.

"Here you are." Mahi was back with the jewelry. "Do smoky eyes like you did for my anniversary." The baby monitor buzzed, indicating Riya was up. Mahi handed

Trisha the pair of diamond studs and a bracelet, and ran back to her apartment. "Get a real dashing guy and have fun, babes," she shouted before closing the door behind her.

⸺⋅❈⧉❈⋅⸺

DAY 3, EVENING
GURUGRAM, NCR

DK video called a third number that Danish carried and this time Danish answered.

"Where are you, Danish?" DK hissed. The low lights behind his brother's lanky face told him he was in a night club and scoring.

"Brother mine! What is this that I'm hearing? You have ruined our family business and there are high chances that soon we'll be on the streets!"

DK frowned at his red eyes. "Have you been using again? Where have you been for the past two days? And where is that friend of yours? Do you even have any idea what you've done?"

"Don't talk to me like that, loser!" Danish chuckled smoking a cigarette.

"Where were you and where is that dealer with whom you have been fraternizing?" DK paced the length of his classy office, while Danish smirked at him again. His lack of respect was putting DK in a mad frenzy.

"He is not a dealer. He is my friend. And he has a name!" Danish grounded his teeth. "His name is Sameer."

"So, where is this Sameer of yours? He should be a pillar of support when we are in dire straits. Because, if he is not around, you are the one who will be answerable to me."

"Answerable to you? Huh!" Danish smirked. "We'll just see." Danish pulled out his phone from his pocket and dialed a number. No one picked up. He dialed again, getting increasingly agitated. His hands trembled as he dialed the number for the third time. "What's wrong with you? Pick up the phone! Pick up the phone, dammit!"

"He is not going to answer. He was an agent. He's gone. Poof! You let a fox in amidst us, you idiot!" DK's other phone rang. It was Jadhav. "Okay, just keep your gab shut," DK said as he answered the call.

Jadhav's voice came on over the speaker. "It was a sabotage at most of the warehouses."

"What kind?" DK asked in a bland tone, the pulse ticking on his jaw.

"The person knew his chemistry. He used whatever was in the godowns and strategically placed the material to blow up the facilities. Two of our night staff dead, and seven drivers are badly injured."

"He must have died in the fire!" Danish cried, "My friend, my loyal friend died because of me. I had given him a room near the central warehouse. He had nowhere to go and I asked him to stay there. Oh my God!" He trembled and slipped down to the floor.

"Cut the drama, Danish." Glancing at him with pure hatred, DK turned to Jadhav. "Where is he?"

"I'm unable to find him. No one has seen him since that night."

"Jadhav is unable to find him because he was the mole, an agent! Do you hear me Danish?" DK shouted.

The phone in Danish's hand trembled as he lifted his head from the table where he had lined up the powder to be inhaled. "How? How do you know this?"

"Nayak called. Your friend is behind all this. If you really value your life Danish, you go under and don't get caught."

"If he has really done what you say then I'll never forgive him. You will have his head, brother. I swear on the half chromosome that we share."

"You aren't supposed to do anything, Danish. The information is as good as gold. You can't do anything, you good for nothing worm! Stay put where you are. You are not supposed to handle anything." DK disconnected the call and blocked his half-brother.

⟶•≼◉▷•⟵

DAY 3. NIGHT
AMRITSAR. PUNJAB

Not supposed to handle anything! How could Sameer do that to me? Took me for a ride, that too for full two years. Danish seethed, exercising at the gym at his friend's house. His long hair was spread on his back, drenched in sweat. Despite all the drug abuse, and the fact that he had become a shadow of his original self, he could bench press for quite some time.

And big brother had trusted Sameer too, and had involved him in the business! And now he is pontificating as if all of it is my mistake. Fucker! Everyone in his life was a bloody actor. Right from his mother, who abandoned him, leaving him to his father who never thought he was capable of anything and left everything to that oaf, DK.

Danish had been just a non-participating entity in the whole business, surviving on crumbs father and DK threw at him. Nowhere did his name appear in black and white. No one gave him the respect due to him.

In a way, it was good though. No one in law enforcement was looking at him now. His image as a Casanova, druggie, and the no-good offspring of a drug linchpin had left him free. Yes, he had been caught under possession quite a number of times but his dear father, then his big, controlling, brother always bailed him out. DK thought he could take charge of the entire empire and give him just handouts in the garb of pocket money.

What DK didn't know was that Danish had been siphoning out money and had accumulated quite a sum in an overseas account. He still had a loyal team who had some serious skills in important areas needed to start any business.

But first, he had to find and kill Sameer. And Danish would show everyone. He'd show all of them what he was capable of. He would take his revenge on everyone who had wronged him. Sameer, then DK.

Fuck family and fuck friends.

Danish pushed his limits on the bench press and made plans.

⋯⋯⋯

CHAPTER FOUR

Armaan tugged at his collar feeling claustrophobic in the black-tie affair that was mandatory for today's soiree. Though he had come back after a long absence, he wanted to run away from all the conventions and rules that bound him to genteel society.

His friend's sister's wedding reception was not his idea of fun. In fact, attending any party was sheer torture for him—formal clothes and polite small talk were not his forte. He had come only out of respect for his friend and to put Karan and Rao at ease that there was nothing wrong with him.

He took a sip of his sparkling water, and calmly studied the crowd. It was quite a gathering—anyone who was someone was in attendance. His best friend at IB and a key part of his rescue team, Junaid, present with his wife, was talking to someone from the tech department. Rao, their boss, was deep in discussion with the home minister. Karan was hitting on beautiful Sharlee, their colleague in the IB's cyber-team, and she sportingly humored him.

Armaan was able to place almost everyone from their team, except their partners—pretty ladies dressed in their fineries—and a few male guests. There were quite a few, since it was the CJI's daughter's wedding reception.

Another reason he had agreed to attend this function was just to wine and dine in style, to counter and forget his two years of exile where he got either cold food or no food at all. The added benefit was meeting the team members who had worked behind the scenes and helped him for the past two years.

Now that he had met everyone who mattered, had eaten enough to last him a lifetime, he didn't have any compelling reason to stay. He wanted to go home and read a horror novel without perpetually looking over his shoulder. He was tired and wanted some quiet after all the mundane conversation. But it was too early. Rao and Dr. Raphel, the department's psychiatrist, would think he was withdrawing in his shell again, so he continued to linger.

To distract himself from the urge to run away, he began to concentrate on the hall decor. It looked like the banquet hall was recently re-modeled on modern lines. The false ceiling was done in random geometrical shapes created using a combination of wood and Plaster-of-Paris. The high walls, clad in Egyptian marble, had hidden crevices with tasteful, concealed lighting in muted colors, adorned with modern art. A portion of the wall to the left of the hall had a glass partition that gave a glimpse of the cool and calm swimming pool outside.

His eyes habitually scanned the view outside the hall and did a double-take. A figure in a black dress stood at the edge of the pool. Slim calves encased in multiple, thin, copper straps of her heels invited him like no other. She stood pensively staring at the water shimmering in the pool. Curiosity had him peeling himself from where he stood in a corner of the hall and start toward the exit leading to the pool.

Maybe he would get lucky in all the aspects today.

Without taking his eyes off her, he exited the big room. She appeared to be deep in her thoughts staring at the blue water that rippled with the slight garden breeze.

"Hope you are not thinking of diving in?"

She gasped and turned around. "Beg your pardon!" Her eyes big on her lean face.

He couldn't help but smile at her 'convent-educated' reaction. The yellow garden lights cast pale shadows on her face making her look enigmatic and royal. Tall and slim with a shoulder-length bob-cut framing her delicate face, she was almost his height in the sexy, foot-breaking heels. He was not used to women matching his height.

"Just curious. You have been staring at the pool for quite some time. I wondered if you were having some self-destructive thoughts." He smiled. The water in the pool was just two feet deep.

A shapely eyebrow arched sophisticatedly. "And you decided to come to my rescue?"

"No... no... please carry on." He waved his glass in the air. "I have no intention of becoming a knight."

"Wouldn't that be anti-climactic since you sought me out to save me from my untimely demise?" Her eyes changed from being pensive to playful.

He suppressed a smile at the encouraging transformation. "So you do believe in heroes, in this era and age!" His own eyes glinted with an answering whimsy.

"It's up to the knight to make me believe in heroes."

"So you are willing to take a chance?"

Ready with an answering retort, she opened her mouth, but her phone rang. She exhaled, threw an exasperated glance at him as if annoyed at the disruption, and answered, "Yes… yes, of course, I'm coming." She looked at him and stepped around, "If you'll excuse me."

He inclined his head, and she left.

Trisha glanced out at the swimming pool. The man who had sought her out had taken her position beside the pool and stood staring at the water, probably with the same expression that she had donned a while ago. He looked a little forlorn clad in a tux which was a shade loose on him. Still, the way he carried himself, she could make out his wide shoulders and quiet strength.

In her many years in college then at the hospital, several men had tried to catch her attention but he was an original. '… no intention of becoming a knight. Really?!' she muttered as a faint smile sneaked on her lips.

Five minutes later, for the very first time in her life, she found herself checking out the man a second time. He was now inside the hall with a couple of men like him—tall, lean and confident in their skin—and a heavily pregnant lady. All of them were standing near the bar, seemingly engaged in some light-hearted banter, because he suddenly threw his head back and laughed. She found her gaze riveted to his face and the pleasant transformation the smile brought to his otherwise grave countenance.

Exactly at that moment, he turned and looked straight at her. Her heart skipped a beat. She should have looked away, but she couldn't. He raised his glass in a silent greeting and took a sip. Unable to break away from his arresting gaze, Trisha's heart raced into unknown territory—a little wicked, a little exciting.

Someone placed a hand on his arm and he turned away releasing her from his spell. She glanced at her phone as if it was a foreign object in her hand. What had happened there? Who was he?

"You okay?" Udit asked.

"Yes, of course."

"You look peaked. Why don't you have something to drink and enjoy a bit?" He picked up a drink from a passing waiter's tray and pushed the cocktail glass in her hand.

⸻ ❖ ⸻

"You need rest, Armaan," Dr. Raphel singled him out when he returned to the hall. "Complete separation from work for at least one month and no brooding alone."

"I never brood." He looked at the short man in specs with a French beard which allegedly hid a weak chin, a pet department joke.

"I have given my recommendations on your psych evaluation results to Rao. He is also like you all, obsessed with work. Hasn't come back with a response."

"*You* told him and *he* didn't listen! You are losing your touch, doc," Armaan teased Dr. Raphel, even as his eyes followed the slow progress of the tall figure in the black dress, on the arm of none other than the head of a famous private hospital chain, Dr. Udit Gaekwad. Not mingling with anyone, she just stood by Gaekwad without uttering a single sentence—like a slave. Maybe she was a companion or an arm candy.

"I'll follow up with him again," Dr. Raphel said.

"Don't bother. I've applied for a fortnight's leave."

"Great. What are you planning to do?"

"Trekking." He watched the girl smile prettily at something Gaekwad said before he steered her by the elbow toward another group.

"I wouldn't recommend it."

He rolled his eyes. "Please don't start a session here, Doc."

"You should find a partner and go with her."

He chuckled. "I didn't know you had this medicine on your prescription."

"Go to Goa or some such place with a girl. Live a little, relax," Dr. Raphel insisted.

"Is he pestering you?" Junaid approached them with his pretty, eight months pregnant wife. "Who is that girl with Gaekwad?" Junaid asked. Udit Gaekwad was now in deep conversation with the home minister.

"Anu, he is ogling other women." Armaan clinked his glass with Anu's.

"Don't worry, I have him on a tight leash. He is only allowed to watch." Anu hugged Junaid's arm and smiled up at him as he nuzzled her temple.

"No seriously, who is she?" Junaid repeated.

The girl in question seemed to be holding her own in the conversation now. Armaan had to rethink his impression of her. Not a companion. Or maybe Gaekwad was too polite and had pulled her into the discussion.

"Who are you talking about?" Karan joined them too.

"That woman with Gaekwad. Have you seen her around?"

"Nope."

Armaan took a sip and rested his eyes on her again. Somehow, her elegant bearing did fit with Gaekwad's personality. If she was an escort, he wouldn't have brought her here. Though he was a loose character, he was discreet and tonight, there were quite a number of members from the media and press, and his sister was around too.

"If she is single, she is perfect for you, Armaan," Dr. Raphel said following Armaan's gaze.

Junaid choked on his drink and sputtered. Anu thumped his back and grinned.

"Wow, Doc, you are matchmaking now. This day will go down in the history of IB," Karan said.

Armaan smiled as Dr. Raphel retained his poker face.

"No, really, or are you changing your profession, Doc? Moving into sex-therapy?" Junaid too tried to pull his leg.

Dr. Raphel ignored them and stared at Armaan. Nobody could ruffle the doctor's calm demeanor, ever. "You know you don't need medicine. Just rest—physically and mentally. And of course, companionship."

Junaid laughed. "He's got his teeth on you, Armaan. You'll have to get laid and give him a summary."

Their repartee was interrupted by a sudden commotion at the exit. The home minister was leaving, and his whole entourage had jumped into action as they ushered him out.

Junaid, Karan, and Armaan came to attention as Rao approached their group.

"Doc. Anu, how are you? Doing good?"

She smiled and nodded.

"At ease, boys."

Armaan winced. Rao had been calling them boys for the past ten years. Armaan felt so old.

"How is it? Enjoying yourself?"

"Yes, Sir," Junaid replied when Armaan just nodded.

"Armaan, I have sanctioned your leave for the next one month. Where are you planning to go? Back to Chandigarh?"

"Yes sir, for a couple of days, then to Laddakh," he replied.

"I don't second it," Dr. Raphel said, "he should be amongst people, friends and company."

"I like my own company," Armaan insisted. He felt like a whining child when he sensed Karan's watchful eyes on him.

"You should listen to Doc. We can't have you decommissioned at your prime," Rao patted his shoulder and moved to another group waiting for his attention.

Armaan scanned the hall again for the girl in black but had no success finding her. She was missing and so was Gaekwad. The band was back on the stage again. They struck the first chord of a song he liked, but a strange aftertaste of betrayal lingered in his mind and he wasn't able to enjoy it.

Trisha was feeling good. The second drink had done the trick, and she was in that zone where the only thing that mattered was her own enjoyment. Mahi was right. The vow she had taken at her father's death could be resumed on Monday. In any case, she couldn't continue the mission here. All the answers were at the hospital, so why not enjoy the moment without thinking of her responsibilities for once. Forgetting everything for one single night should not matter when the mission had had her attention for years. Tonight, she'd be a little selfish. Tonight was for her.

The party bored her though. She didn't know anyone besides Udit and he had gone somewhere with one of the hospital board's directors. Priya was also around but she was surrounded by the high and mighty of the society and didn't even acknowledge Trisha.

Trisha found herself walking out of the hall and to the pool again. As expected, no one was around. A bit disappointed, she stared at the shimmering water again. What had she hoped for? She didn't know. Or maybe she knew. She wanted to meet him again. She looked through the glass wall inside the hall but she couldn't spot him inside either. A little disheartened, she turned toward the exit from the gardens and stopped short.

"Still waiting for a hero?" he asked, hands in his pockets, leaning on the wall near the door to the hall, a little smug in his skin. With that faint smile bordering on arrogance, he looked devastatingly good. To her. Wicked good. *Control yourself,* the voice of sanity muttered somewhere in her mind.

Trisha had to admit he had had an upper hand in the conversation so far. She had to make amends. "I'm not in dire straits or a damsel in distress. A hero would be wasted with me."

"Heroes can help beat boredom too." He grinned.

He had such a killer smile. Gosh! The left incisor and the tooth beside it were slightly crooked, and a dimple peeked on his right cheek. She had an unscrupulous desire to run her fingers through his thick brown hair, instead she curled them on her clutch and said, "I'm not bored."

"Liar," he breathed softly as his eyes crinkled on the edges.

Something tugged at the beats inside her heart. She wanted the conversation to continue. "How?" she asked, flicking back to his question on boredom earlier.

"By dancing to the right tune." He smiled as he spoke, and held out his hand toward her, totally in tune with her thoughts.

"Here?" The tug was harder this time. Her heart tingled and stomach tightened. She felt a faint flush rising on the side of her neck, as she glanced at him then at his hand. *Not a good idea,* the voice of sanity warned.

"Why not?" He smiled as the band drummed in regular fast beats, signaling the start of a new song.

She exhaled and placed her hand in his. He pulled her into his arms, a little too close for comfort, but his hard strength, head to toe, warmed her to the core.

The warm twinkling lights threw sieved shadows on them transporting them into a utopian world, where only the two of them breathed and existed. She didn't know if he too felt the same, but his mood seemed to blend well with her quixotic self. When the heat between them became too much, she focused her attention on something behind him. *Impulsive, insane*, the voice of sanity blurted, but Trisha was past caring. This was for her. Only for her.

"Are you attached to that man back there? Or, for that matter to anyone?"

She shook her head and closed her eyes, as the magic of the moment engulfed her.

"I'm Armaan," he said when the song finished and another began.

She raised her eyes to his dreamy ones. Armaan. Desire. His name too had an exotic lilt to it. But she didn't want any personal association to this night. "Are introductions really necessary?" she asked.

A brow went up. "No, not at all," he said.

Amused as well as intrigued, Armaan watched the dancing yellow lights from the garden and the hall on her face. So she wanted the charade to be played in anonymity? He would be a mad man to disagree with her.

Her eyes fell on his lips, then lowered down to concentrate on his neck. He wondered if his tie was knotted incorrectly. The faint urge to impress her surprised him. A lot.

She was a bit under the influence, but not so much to lose control. Her curious eyes scanned his face with concealed interest. In her heels, she was almost as tall as him so he could look straight into her deep, caramel colored eyes, wreaking havoc on his senses.

The music came to a halt, but he couldn't step back. She looked at him when he couldn't let go. His eyes then dropped to her lips. A little flustered, she ran her tongue over her lip and blood took a deep dive from his brain to his groin.

"I have a room here," he said softly. Not exactly the truth, but he had resources. One call and a room would be available without any questions asked.

"Not a good idea."

"Take a risk." He tightened his hold on her waist. "With me."

"I don't think I'm that bored," she whispered.

"You don't know what you want."

An eyebrow went up. "A little presumptuous of you, don't you think?"

Armaan watched her delicate features and copper-colored shoulder-skimming locks. A faint sheen of perspiration coated her fair forehead. She was nervous. "Probably not, but what's a hero without any spontaneity? Anything to woo the beautiful damsel and save her from boredom." He pressed on, "If it eases your mind, I am one of the most respectable people around. Come on, I would have never guessed you would chicken out of an adventure."

"You think of this as an adventure?"

"Risky things normally are." He slid his hand from her waist down to her hip, pulling her closer. "Adventurous and pleasurable."

He watched the struggle between her heart and her mind. And he knew the exact moment when her heart won.

⸻ ◈◈◈ ⸻

CHAPTER FIVE

By force of habit, Armaan had scoped the entire hotel already and knew the floor plans and exits by heart. He took her from the back entrance to the elevators lobby, simultaneously texting his contact. By the time they entered the elevator, he had received a response with the room number. He pressed the button for the seventh floor and then glanced at her.

She was standing on the far side of the elevator cabin, hands clutching the mid-height cabin bars, putting as much distance as she could between them. They looked at each other and the air between them smoldered. Though he was very clear about what he wanted, he knew she was having doubts. The degree of attraction between them was the only thing that bound them that evening and that was the only thing that mattered. Tomorrow would come the next day.

The elevator came to a stop before he could ask her name. They stood apart even when the doors opened.

"Do you want to step out, Sir? Ma'am?" A waiter stood outside holding a tray in one hand and the elevator door with the other.

She stepped out without a word and he followed her.

"You okay?" he asked when he reached the room.

"Er… yeah… "

He clicked open the room. "I… just want you to know that whenever you want to put a stop to this, I'll stop." He closed the door behind them.

She stepped forward scanning the room.

"Do you want a drink?" he asked. Suddenly it struck him that he wanted to know more about her before the final act.

"No." She ran her hands on the sofa back, then looked everywhere but at him.

He stepped toward her and took her in his arms again. "Do you hear the melodious music playing or am I the only one intoxicated?"

She let out a low laugh, when he swayed with the seductive silence, taking her with him. "Yes, I do. But how will an intoxicated knight rescue a damsel in distress?"

"This one rescues better when intoxicated." The magic from the pool below swirled and entered the room in seconds. He lifted a hand and tucked her hair behind her ear. "Are we good?"

Trisha was impressed with his chivalry. He was giving her time to back out if she was having second thoughts. No, there were no thoughts in her mind, leave aside second or third, except that she wanted his hand on every inch of her bare body. "Yes, we're good." Ignoring the faint voice of sanity that was now pushed and smothered into a corner of her mind by her raging hormones, she leaned forward and placed her lips on his.

Damn! He smelled so good and her entire body seemed to melt in his, as his palm slid down her arm to her waist. A sound of pleasure, humming in his throat, he let her kiss him for a few seconds then changed gears and took control. All her nerve endings screamed for closer contact. God, she had been so lonely!

When his mouth found hers again—hot, smooth, and sweet—she forgot everything except the sensation he invoked in her. Closing her eyes, she angled her head to give him free access to her neck. He bit her lip and moved down, caressing and kneading her waist and down to her hips. Trailing small kisses on her neck, nape, he turned her around.

Nibbling the feverish skin on her shoulders, he cupped her breast. She moaned as her thumbs flicked over her nipples sending a spear of heat straight down her knees. Her dress was somehow loose... then she realized he had pulled down the zip. His hands skimmed over her bare shoulders as he slipped the strap down on her arm.

"You are lovely," he whispered as the dress pooled down to her ankles and she stepped out of the garment. The strapless, silky, black bra was next to be taken off. Feeling a little shy, she turned around and mirrored his actions. Slipping down his coat off his shoulders, she loosened his tie and slipped it over his head. Her hands trembled over the buttons of his shirt, so much so that he had to help her and soon even the shirt was discarded.

Flicking her chin up, he leaned in and took her mouth. Warm and soft, she stumbled as her legs refused to support her. Gently and surely, he backed her to the bed and they tumbled down on the soft sheet—mouth to mouth, chest to nipples, legs entwined. Skillful, tender play of lips, gentle scrape of his five o'clock shadow.

Breathing hard and wanting closer contact, her hands went to his belt. He shifted and lifted, helped her, then himself. She groaned and buried her face in his neck as the last of the barriers were removed between them.

He held her for a minute as if savoring the sheer moment of pleasure then began the last assault. Sunk deep in the bed, she let him take, as much as he gave her. His hands strong, capable, and seductively unfamiliar. Their bodies adjusting to the new sinful planes and curves, and fitting just right.

A quick pounding of the pulse. A delicious shiver of ecstasy. Both their hearts began to thunder as the need to scale the peak began to thrum in the blood. The last thought in her mind before she was lost in the mind-blowing orgasm was—oh my! how could she have lived without it for so many years!

⬤•≺⊹◈⊹≻•⬤

Trisha was comfortable—too comfortable—on the silky white, soft sheets twisting all around her. Something warm and heavy, like the stuffed boa constrictor she owned as a child, was draped on her waist. She pushed at the toy on her waist and it grunted softly. Her eyes snapped open and the night's memories came rushing.

'Oh God! What had she done?!' The first thought went to the most practical thing—fear of pregnancy. But that was okay it was the wrong time of the month and he had used a condom. She closed her eyes again. Never had she been in a situation like this, even when she was a teenager, vulnerable to instant attraction.

When her heart settled a bit and acknowledged her uncharacteristic, irresponsible behavior, she prepared herself to face the consequences. Clutching the soft silk sheet up to her neck, she opened her eyes in a slit and peeked at him again. He was still there, sleeping—peaceful and oblivious. She opened her eyes and stared at the handsome face that showed a deeper hint of the five o'clock shadow on his chiseled jaw. Hair all tousled, her night's work, he was sleeping with one arm above his head. Gosh! He was delicious!

Sometime in the past hours, one of them had pulled the duvet over them, she couldn't remember who. The sheets too were entangled all around them. They had reached out to each other more than once in the past hours. Her whole body warmed at the recollection. 'Get real, Trish.' She willed herself to cool down. Slowly and steadily, she pulled the sheet and thankfully, it came off without disturbing him.

Easing away from his hold, she clutched the sheet securely around her, leaving the duvet on him. The time on her mobile phone showed it was three in the morning. Their clothes scattered all over the plush room—her dress, his shirt, his tie on her sandals—made her blush again. Gathering her things quickly, she made her way to the bathroom. She didn't look into the mirror as she washed his scent off and donned her clothes.

Thankful of the fact that at such posh hotels the doors didn't creak, she stepped out of the bathroom fully dressed. As quietly as she could, Trisha picked up her purse, phone, and her heels. Bare feet, she tiptoed out of the room.

The import of her reckless behavior hit Trisha hard when she reached the privacy of her room at home. Tushar was still at Mahi's. She sat down on the bed with her head in her hands.

What was it about him that had caused her to lose all sense of the decorum she had followed throughout her life? After the untimely death of her father ten years ago, life had thrown her into the thick of responsibilities and she had never lost control over her senses like the way she did last night.

The only saving grace was that she hadn't given him her name. It was highly unlikely that they would meet again. Her naughty night of reckless entertainment was over. She had to put the episode behind her.

——————

Armaan had never been so comfortable. A fantastic night with a beautiful woman did that to a man who had not had a decent, clean bed for two years running, leave aside sleeping with a warm, soft body. As the last dregs of sleep and lethargy left him, Armaan reached out to take her into his arms again, even before he opened his eyes. But his hands only found the cool and mussed sheets.

His eyes snapped open. He turned his head and indeed he was sleeping alone. Lifting his head, he scanned the room. The bathroom door was closed. Maybe she was in there. He closed his eyes and lay back again.

When she didn't come out of the bathroom after a reasonable passage of time, he got up and knocked on the bathroom door. There was no response. He pushed the door and it swung open slightly. He peeked inside. She wasn't there.

It took him a minute to search the room, bathroom and the balcony, and another thirty to accept that she had indeed left without a single… damn… What was he expecting? A parting note? A message? He lunged at his phone. There were no texts or calls from unknown numbers.

But why?

She hadn't even given him her name! Why? Why had she insisted on being anonymous? His mind ran into all kinds of possibilities including several conspiracy theories. Had someone sent her specifically after him? No. No. He shouldn't think like that! Doc would put him under PTSD watch. She could have murdered him ten times last night. God knows she had ample opportunity since he had behaved like a besotted fool all night, worshipping her body.

As he dressed and left the room, he realized he didn't want a one-night stand with her. He wanted more. He could look at the hotel's camera feed and could find out everything about her in two hours' time, but he was not in a habit of pursuing women who didn't want his attention. No. On second thought, he won't look for her. Ever.

He shook his head as he hailed a cab.

Even after the firm resolve, he still felt like a jilted Romeo.

⊶❖⊷

Trisha preferred the night shift on Friday and had offered to be on a twenty-four-hour call duty on Saturday too, filling in for a colleague. The night shift was perfect for her to resume her sleuthing at the hospital. No matter how much the Dragon tried to keep an eye over everything in the OT and the ICU, she had to take rest and that gave Trisha ample opportunity to carry out her plan.

Trisha had already marked all the CCTV cameras and their span of reach. She had figured out a route to the main office where all the surgery records were kept without being spotted on a camera feed. Today, she was going to search the small room off the green doors on the top floor, the keys to which were in the Dragon's office.

Trisha watched the Dragon crooning to Udit as he came out of the ICU after his evening rounds. Throughout the day, Trisha had managed to do her own work without drawing undue attention to herself and now she was on the floor for a consult. They discussed something in hushed tones, then the Dragon nodded twice and went out of the ICU.

"Hey, Trisha, wassup?" Udit asked.

"I just wanted your opinion on one of my patients." She smiled and held out a file.

"Yeah, sure." After explaining to her the next course of action, which she already knew, he too left the nursing station of the ICU.

It was eleven, when Trisha went around the chest of drawers, pretending to write something, and when she knew she was out of the camera range, she ducked down behind the drawers. Crouching down, she hobbled behind the nurses' L-shaped desk and entered Ms. Paul's office. She pulled out a drawer that had a bunch of keys. She had done this many a times. The keys would not be missed till the next morning.

She went back the way she had come and stood up near the chest of drawers. Except for a new nurse who was taking out something from the medicine cabinet, no one had witnessed her foray into the Dragon's lair.

Trisha looked at the keys in her hand. Two computers in the room were the only place she hadn't checked. After this, if she didn't find the list, then it was not in this facility.

She quickly switched on the computer and keyed in the password she had deciphered after watching Ms. Paul carefully for many months. It had been quite simple as Paul had only a couple of combinations of passwords that she used all over the hospital.

The moment she logged into one of the two computers, she heard the footsteps. Heart pounding, she switched off the screen and crouched under the table. Two shadows fell on the thin line of light under the door. Someone wearing shoes had stopped in front of the door. With the help of the lone chair in the room, Trisha climbed on the metal *almirah* placed along the side wall parallel to the door. She plastered herself to the far side between the ceiling and wall. If someone opened the door they wouldn't be able to spot her.

The person spoke in a hushed tone, perhaps on a phone. Trisha couldn't make out. It seemed he or she was having an argument. The knob twisted and the door opened. The person stopped at the threshold, still holding the phone. After what seemed like an eternity, the door was pulled shut and Trisha heard footsteps walking away from the door. Heart thudding painfully in her chest, she endured the deafening silence on the floor for at least ten minutes, then came down.

After the near miss of being found out and spending over four hours on the two computers, Trisha found only disappointment and dejection. She had been so hopeful that she would find the list here. Taking a deep breath, she exited the record room.

After placing the keys in Ms. Paul's office desk, she hobbled back to the chest of drawers at the nurses' station. Dawn was breaking through the windows of the ward. Blood drained from her face when she found the Dragon staring at her when she stood up. She had thought Ms. Paul was not due till eight a.m.

"What are you doing here, Dr. Mehra?"

Fortunately, when she had been snooping and sleuthing for so many months, Trisha had practiced a lot of excuses she could use in case she was caught. "Well, I was looking for a drug list and my phone fell down." She took a deep, silent breath. Why was she sounding like a naughty child who was caught red-handed by the warden?! Well, she was the warden for all the hospital wards.

"The drug list is not kept here, Dr. Mehra."

"Oh!" Trisha aced the innocent and dumb look.

"Next time, call me if you need anything."

"But you weren't due for another couple of hours."

"Well, I'm here now."

Trisha backed up her excuse with a genuine case for which she needed to look at the drug list. She took the information from Ms. Paul and left the record room, breathing easy only after taking the elevator to the residents' room.

⸻⸻

DAY 6. MORNING
ZENITH HOSPITAL. NEW DELHI

Ms. Paul had to inform Priya about today's clash.

She had been with Udit and Priya for years. In fact, she considered both of them as her children. She had helped them in every phase of their lives, just as they had supported her children and her family, and had made her rich beyond her imagination. So what if they lived a life that didn't conform to society's norm. In Ms. Paul's eyes, they were royals, class apart, who could do nothing wrong.

And Ms. Paul didn't know why Priya was thinking of hooking Dr. Mehra with Udit. She hated Dr. Mehra's guts. Though Mehra appeared subdued and was excellent with the patients, Ms. Paul knew that something was cooking behind those cool, intelligent, bored eyes.

When she couldn't find Priya, she made a beeline to Udit's office on the top floor. She opened the door softly and beamed with pride.

"Susan, what brings you here?" Udit smiled when he spotted her.

"I think she went to the record room today."

"Who?"

"Dr. Trisha Mehra."

"Oh!" Udit frowned. "What was she doing there?"

"I didn't find her there, but on the floor at the nurses' station. Made some excuse about a drug list and said her phone fell down."

"Then it must be that, Susan. You are getting unnecessarily worked up."

"But Udit—"

"It's okay. Keep an eye on her. I'll ask Marathe for the security camera feed and check her comings and goings myself."

That satisfied Ms. Paul and she left pleased with herself.

The door to Udit's office opened again. Annoyed, he lifted his eyes, then smiled. "Hey."

"Hey to you too." Priya entered and closed the door behind her.

His sister stood at the threshold of the room in a plain green silk ensemble looking every inch the diva he and the rest of the world thought she was. He was so proud of her that it seemed his chest would explode. "I thought you had an off today."

"Yes. But I was feeling very restless so I thought should spend some time with you, now that your surgeries are over."

"Yes. Come on in. Shall I ring for Ms. Paul to bring some herbal tea for you?"

"No, Udit. I just wanted to see your face." She brushed her hand over his shoulders and stayed there. "You settle me down."

"I'm always here, sweetheart." He placed his palm on her hand.

⸻

CHAPTER SIX

"I think, I'll just lie down here and chill." Armaan switched the channel again.

Karan looked at his big brother, who needed to put on some meat on his bones. He had been nagging Armaan for the past four days to make some plan that required them to step out of the apartment, but he hadn't been successful.

"Are you still pining for that girl? What had exactly happened?" he couldn't help and finally asked. As per the rules of the brotherly Bible, they were not supposed to discuss each other's night outs with a woman. "I thought I'd see you Monday morning when I saw you pulling her into the lobby Saturday night."

"Crashed and burned." Armaan raised the volume of the TV.

"What happened?" Karan couldn't let go.

"She left before I woke up."

"Her loss," Karan replied.

"Thanks for the vote of confidence, bro," Armaan said and changed the channel again.

A screeching song in some foreign language filled up the living room, making the brothers wince. Armaan quickly changed the channel again to hear a journalist screaming into the microphone. Karan snatched the remote control and reduced the volume.

"It will do you good to meet people and generally socialize."

The corners of Armaan's lips twitched at the tone Karan had taken.

"Don't laugh."

"Do you see me laughing, Mom?" Armaan grinned.

"We need to go shopping."

Armaan groaned.

"Come on. You need to buy new clothes. You've shrunk and look like a hanger in everything old. And I too need a few things."

"You are always needing things, fashion plate."

"I have to look good, else how will I attract the right kind of attention." Karan narrowed his eyes at the reflective surface of the coffee table and swiped his palm on his jaw, angling it this way and that. "Boy, is anybody as handsome as me?"

"Cut it out, lover boy. There's no one here to applaud your vanity."

"But we are going shopping. Remember how the suit at the party looked unflattering on you? We didn't have the time for a replacement then, but we have it now, so giddy up, my man and come to war."

Armaan knew he didn't stand a chance when Karan was in that mood and grudgingly obliged.

⸻❖⸻

DAY 10. AFTERNOON
SAKET MALL. NEW DELHI

Trisha took a rare one hour off from the hospital on Wednesday and went to a mall nearby. She had to buy some everyday clothes and replace her running gear. As she was trying on the clothes she had picked, she heard a familiar drawl from the other cubicle. Blood seemed to have frozen in her veins as the husky voice registered in her mind and her heartbeats boomed in her chest. Was it really him? No, no. This serendipity could not be happening to her.

It seemed that the ladies' cubicle shared a wall with men's. Losing all interest in trying out the new clothes, she strained to hear his voice. It came again. Two men were seemingly having some kind of argument over the fit. Then she heard someone call out the name. Armaan.

Oh, God! He was actually here. Only a wall separated them. What was he doing here? And why today, why now! She was in no position to face him. Oh God, why did she pick up this day of all the days? She wouldn't come to this mall ever!

She could leave the store immediately. But what if he too came out and noticed her in the store? She could hide till he left. Or, since he seemed busy inside she could sneak out of the trial room, then out of the store, and finally out of the mall. She wouldn't look back.

She left the clothes in the cubicle and peeked out of the little cabin, except for a couple of teenagers in the adjacent stall, no one was about. She tip-toed out of the trial rooms' section, keeping her head down, and left the store and the mail without buying a single damn thing. She took a deep breath only after the elevator doors closed with her inside.

What the feck?!

Why was he here? Did he live nearby? Would they meet again? What if he came to her hospital someday? Oh, why did she do the thing that she did that night? What was she thinking?

DAY 10, AFTERNOON
SAKET MALL, NEW DELHI

Karan's phone rang while Armaan was paying the bill.

"What happened?" Armaan asked after Karan disconnected the call.

"I have to go to the office. There has been some development in a case. Take the car, Junaid is nearby and is coming to pick me up. I'll take a cab later."

Nodding Armaan and Karan went their separate ways. Armaan went down to the basement parking and Karan toward the exit gate.

Tugging at the neck of his T-shirt, Armaan opened the second button and exited the lift to the lower basement parking. For a moment he just stood there realizing he had forgotten to ask Karan about the bay where they had parked the car. The problem one faces when one comes back to civilization after a long time.

The parking area was huge, and the bays were segregated by the colors of the pillars in between. He remembered noticing the blue pillars when they had parked and walked toward the blue area, clicking on the car key. There she was! His shiny new black beauty winked at him as he pressed the key again. A smile appeared involuntarily on his face.

He took a step toward the car and sensed a movement between his car and the one parked adjacent to it. By force of habit, his hands went to his absent shoulder holster, panic raised his heckles. The next second he remembered that he had strapped the gun to his ankle and sighed in relief. "Hey, what are you doing?" A girl in black crouched on the floor.

The woman gasped and stood up quickly. There was a collective intake of breath as their eyes met. The woman from the party, the one who left him sleeping without a by your leave, stood in front of him vaguely gesturing toward the floor.

"Er… I… I have dropped my keys somewhere here." She stood there pinching her pinkie finger of her left hand, her eyes darting here and there in panic.

He stared at her in confusion, anger, and relief.

"Umm… I'm sorry," she mumbled, her fair face flaming.

"What are you sorry for?" His hands fisted by his side.

"Er…" She cleared her throat. "I've to find my car keys."

He looked at her car and then at his own. His pleasure went down a few notches. Her's was way out of his league.

"If you would be kind enough to move your car, I'll be able to go home." Arms around her middle, she looked at everything but him.

"You are not going anywhere till we have a civilized discussion about that night. But first of all, tell me your na—" He took a step to the driver's side and heard a familiar faint sound—the swo…osh of air being displaced. He dived between the two cars, taking her with him.

"Ouch… what the—! What are you doing?" She struggled under him, pushing at his chest.

"Shh…shh." He put one hand on her mouth and held her head lightly with the other. Head tilted at an angle, he tried to listen again. "Didn't you hear the sound?" he muttered. She shook her head frantically behind his hand, her eyes wide with fear. "Just be quiet. Don't shout okay? I'm lifting my hand." He released her when she nodded emphatically and took out his gun.

"What's wrong with you? I didn't hear a thing," she whispered massaging her elbow. Her eyes went wide again when she noticed the gun in his hand.

"Someone took a shot at us," he whispered back. He tried to peer through the windows of the car. The pillar beyond their two cars gave them adequate cover.

"Shot? What! I didn't hear a thin—"

"He is using a silencer." She tried to get up, but he pulled her down and hissed, "I said don't get up!"

She peered closely into his eyes. "You are nuts. Are you drunk?" she whispered and then cleared her throat and spoke normally, "Let me get up."

"No, stay put for a few minutes. I'll scout around. Okay?" He shook her by her shoulders when she just lay there staring incredulously at him. "Did you hear me? Don't get up or leave. We have to talk."

She frowned but nodded.

He went crouching around the pillar, trying to gauge the angle of the shot and the likely trajectory. He scanned the entire car park from his position. There was no unusual movement or sound. The bullet must be embedded in the cement walls or the pillars since the ground was level and there was no apparent damage to any other car.

"Nothing." Coming back the same way he had gone, he addressed her delectable backside.

She was trying to find her keys under his car using her cell phone torch. "Thank god!" She spotted her keys next to his car's tire and picked them up. "You have ruined my top."

The fabric at the back was torn beyond repair and was hanging on one side, exposing the silk lining. A bruise was also forming on her elbow. He didn't mention that at all.

She tried to straighten up again, but he held her down. He took a deep breath and kept his voice low. "Don't get up. Just stoop and enter the car with your head down."

She looked into his eyes again. This time, she tried to part his eyelids.

He shrank back. "What are you doing?"

"Looking at the dilation of your pupils. I'm a doctor," she said.

He looked at her serious black eyes, straight pert nose, and soft mouth, and experienced the familiar exquisite ache. No matter what she wanted, it was not going to be a one-night stand between them, he knew for sure.

A group of young women came out of the elevators and walked toward an SUV parked nearby, breaking the churn of hormones between them.

"You might be having some serious problem. I think you are hallucinating," she said.

She was so serious that despite the situation he began to smile. "Just… enter from this side… and keep your head as low as possible, then follow my car. We will talk over a cup of coffee and discuss my condition."

She clenched her jaw but shrugged and followed his instructions while getting into her car. "You should see a doctor. I can give you a reference," she said winding down the car window.

He shook his head and grinned. "Just wait for me to get into my car, then follow me."

To his acute surprise, she started the car and just drove off. What was wrong with her? What part of his instructions did she not understand? He quickly got into his own car and screeched out of the parking lot, but there was no sign of her car outside.

Driving through to Karan's apartment, he replayed the scene again. He was sure he had heard the gun shot even though it was masked by the silencer. He was trained to hear. But there was utter silence after that first sound. And he couldn't locate the bullet in the vicinity, not that he could really look around given the threat, but it could have been lodged anywhere in the parking lot.

Still, he called up Junaid and recounted the situation for him and his location in the parking bay. Junaid promised to send a team immediately to look for any foul play.

Who could be shooting at him? He had worked undercover for his last assignment. No one, absolutely no one, could have recognized him. Was it something to do with one of his older assignments? It couldn't be. Or did he imagine that sound? Was he really losing it? Was she right?

And was she really a doctor or was she just trying to distract him by pulling a fast one? By her reaction, it seemed she had never expected to meet him again. Finding her would be a half an hour's job for the department because he had memorized her car number, but he was so pissed off at her running away that he didn't want to exert any effort or expend the department's resources for her.

To hell with…

***

DAY 10. AFTERNOON
ZENITH HOSPITAL. NEW DELHI

It took Trisha half an hour to relax and stop glancing at the rearview mirror every three seconds. The way he commanded her to drive and follow him, she was sure he would follow her, but probably he got delayed, or maybe she was too fast for him.

On the night of the party, he was so chilled out, but today he was really on the edge. Who was he? Was he in law enforcement? Given that he was attending CJI's party, he could be. Or someone on the other side! 'No need to get fanciful, Trisha Mehra.' She chuckled and entered the hospital parking lot.

***

CHAPTER SEVEN

Uncharacteristic silence greeted Trisha as she opened the lock and entered her apartment late that Friday evening after her emergency duty. Kishore Dada must have convinced Tushar to go off to sleep on time, which was very rare but not unprecedented. She placed the keys in the bowl on the chest of drawers in the entrance lobby and froze. The second set of keys to the house was missing. She heard the click then and turned. Her stomach twisted painfully as her heart sank down into her stomach.

A man—a masked man—stood with his hand on Tushar's mouth and a gun trained on his head. "Any sound and he dies," he said in a low drawl.

Her purse, coat, and stethoscope slid on the floor from her limp hands. Tushar's hands were bound behind his back and tears streamed down his cheeks. A bruise stood out on his left cheek, stark against the white pallor of his face.

Was she facing this because of her snooping at the hospital? Had they come to know? Kishore Dada had warned her that they were dangerous people. Oh my God! Had she brought the danger home? To her brother? And Dada!

"What do you want?" her voice came out in a hoarse whisper, "Please release him. He is just a child. Where's Dada?"

"Just step forward and sit down." The man angled his chin toward the single sofa chair in the corner.

She took a tentative step into the living room and sank on the sofa, and saw the other man by the window. He too was masked and held a gun.

"What is it? What do you want?"

In answer, the one who held Tushar slapped him.

"Don't!" She jostled out of her chair as Tushar whimpered.

"Keep sitting!" the other man snapped, pushing her down into the seat by her shoulders.

Tears sprung into her eyes when Tushar clinched his eyes and mewled like a mute wounded pup. "What do you want? Take everything we have, just don't hit him!"

The man slapped a photo on the coffee table in front.

Her heart raced painfully to see a familiar pair of eyes—Armaan's eyes—staring at her. Oh God! Who was he? Was he connected to the Gaekwads? Was he scoping her out at the party and at the mall?

She stared at the two men. Were they his goons? His bizarre behavior at the parking lot began to make sense. He had a gun on him too. Was a gun really fired, like he kept saying? Had her chance meeting with him brought danger to her brother. Or had she been a target all along, and he knew all about her but was having fun before he brought down this nightmare on her?

"I didn't do anything!" She looked up from the photo to the two men towering over her.

"No, you didn't. But now you will. You will do exactly what we tell you or your brother dies."

"No!" She looked at Tushar. He hadn't opened his eyes and was continuously crying. "Please, please, I'll do anything."

"Think it through, Dr. Mehra. Anything means anything." He ran his hand on her arm, glancing at her in such an obscene way that she cringed back into the sofa cushions.

The man threw his head back and laughed. "Anything can happen, Dr. Trisha Mehra." He then clicked his fingers and waved his hand at his companion, who pulled Tushar toward the bedrooms.

"Wait! Where are you taking him?"

"Keep sitting!"

"Please, please, don't hurt him." It didn't surprise her to feel a tear rolling down her cheek. Her hands cold and stiff in her lap.

"Whether he gets hurt or not depends on your cooperation, Doctor." The man pushed her down into the sofa by her shoulders as the other one took away Tushar to his room and shut the door.

Oh God! Was she going to get raped! No, it looked like they wanted something from her. She had to keep her wits about her—to think of a way to escape or call for help. Where had they taken Dada? He would never abandon Tushar. Had they killed him? She forced herself to breathe deeper as she stared at the photo on the table. Oh, God! Why had she met this man? He looked so handsome and confident. He said he was respectable! All her life she had never entertained any romantic thoughts about anyone and the one time she had…

"So, Dr Mehra, let's talk business." The man sat down on the other side, waving the gun all around. "You seem to know this man. What's his name?" He tapped the photo with the gun.

"I don't know him. I've only met him twice, and that too coincidently."

"His name!" he snapped.

Her eyes jerked to his face by the sheer force of his voice. In a trance, she stared at his black eyes peering through the slits.

"You know his name, Dr Mehra. Don't make me sweat or your brother gets beaten up there."

On clue, she heard Tushar grunt and groan on the other side of the door.

"Armaan," she blurted, "He just told me his first name. Please don't hurt him!"

"What does he do?"

"I don't know! He didn't tell me. I swear he didn't!"

"Okay." He got up and began to pace her small living area, a place where she otherwise found her peace and comfort. It was her safe haven. But now, it was forever ruined for them—Tushar and her.

She could still hear Tushar weeping. Tears ran down her eyes freely now, as she waited for the man to continue the torture with words.

"You have to bring this man to a place near Sukhna Wildlife Sanctuary, without telling him about us or what's happening in this house."

"What? How?"

"Just shut up!" he shouted.

Trisha flinched.

"Listen to me very carefully, Trisha. Can I call you that? Trisha? I think I can. Now that our association will be close and personal, I will call you Trisha. Now pay heed to me. You are going to drive to the national highway tomorrow morning where your car will break down. This man…" he tapped the photo, "…will drive up to you and will help you. You have to convince him to drop you all the way to the address we give you."

"How will I do that? My car is absolutely alright. It's new. Why will he listen to me? He doesn't even know me!" Trisha knew she was babbling. Nothing made sense.

"Don't get ahead, Doc. We will place you in his way, then you just have to act as if you are a damsel in distress and make sure you reach this address…"

Damsel in distress!

God, how she hated that phrase in that moment!

He slapped a piece of paper on top of the photo, "…with him, without telling anything about us or your brother. When you reach the address, you all will be free to go, your brother, you and your servant here." He pointed to kitchen.

Her eyes darted to the kitchen floor then came back to him. "But how will I convince him to come with me? He doesn't know me at all." A minuscule wave of relief anchored her. Dada wasn't dead and they wanted something from her, which had nothing to do with the Gaekwads.

"That's your job, Trisha." He moved behind her.

"What if he is able to fix my car?"

"That's our headache. He won't be able to repair… or do anything to the car." She jumped when he breathed in her ear, his breath on her nape making her hair stand—her heart racing like an athlete.

"Act, improvise, but you have to bring him to this address." He tapped the paper leaning over her shoulder. "If you don't, your brother and your faithful old man dies." He ran a tongue over her ear lobe. She tilted her face away and closed her eyes. "And I will find you and will make sure you are not fit for any man."

Tushar wept behind the door.

"Now!" He snapped from somewhere above her head, making her heart leap in her throat again. "Let's go to your room. We are going to pack for your trip." He caught hold of her elbow in a tight grip and pulled her up, then pushed her toward her room. From the corner of her eye, she saw a pair of legs in the kitchen. "He is old and weak!" she whispered.

"Worry about your brother and yourself, sweetheart."

⋘◆⋙

"You've understood what I want, Doc?"

Slumped on the floor beside her almirah, scared, worried and tired to the bone, she nodded. It was one a.m. in the night and she had not had anything since the cold sandwich at the hospital for lunch. What about Tushar and Dada? Had they given them anything? She hoped they had given them water at least.

The man had made her pack for the weekend. She was supposed to take him to a place on the highway, where he would do something to her car so it would need repairs. Then, she was to wait for Armaan to drive by and ask for his help. And after that—?

After that, she didn't have a clue how she'd convince Armaan to take her to that address near Chandigarh.

"Why will he agree to escort me there?" she asked, "Who is he?"

"You don't have to worry your pretty head about that, darling. Just use your feminine charm and sharp mind and you will find a solution. With so many degrees behind your name, it should be a piece of cake for you. I'm sure you will find a way to lure him. If I read the scene in the parking lot correctly, he is in any case enamored by you." He was lying on her bed waving the gun here and there.

So, he had seen them in the parking lot! What if she lunged at him and snatched the gun? But if she was not quick enough, the man in the next room might kill Tushar. No, she couldn't take that risk.

Trisha shrank back against the wall as he stood up and came toward her. "What happens once we reach there?" She wanted to keep him talking so that his attention was not focused on her. So far she knew she was safe from his unwanted attention, as he didn't want any mark on her before her meeting with Armaan. Still!

"You will get the instructions there."

"What about my brother and Dada?"

"Your brother will also be taken there. You will meet him at the farmhouse. And the old man stays here. My men will free him and leave your house the moment you reach the farmhouse with Armaan."

"I have to talk to my brother every four hours."

He laughed out loud. "You are not in a position to demand anything."

"I have to talk to him, so that I know he is alive and well. Else, I'll have no motivation to do anything." She glared at him.

He cocked his head this way and that, watching her, making her feel extremely uncomfortable but she held his gaze. After a few agonizing seconds, he jerked his head. "You got me there, Doc. Okay, fine. I'll make sure you get to speak to him before all the meals. And now to the next stage."

He got up and picked up the plastic ties he had brought with him, and tied her legs and hands. Then he gagged her using one of her hand towels and went out of the room.

⸎

DAY 13. EARLY MORNING
NOIDA. NCR

All set?" Karan asked coming out of his room.

"Yeah." Armaan zipped close his duffel bag, then stuffed a roll of socks in the side pocket and stood up. "Meet soon."

"Yup."

"When I'm back, come visit me at the cantonment."

"Provided they don't send you on another assignment."

"That is why I asked you to come on the trek with me."

"You know I have to be here. Rao has another assignment for me," Karan said.

"Yeah, I know. And I also know you love your job, so stop whining."

"I hope you meet a pretty, single woman on your trek."

"Thank you." Armaan picked up his backpack and hugged Karan.

"Take care of my bro, okay. See you soon."

"You take care of mine. See you." Armaan saluted and left.

⸺⊱⋇⊰⸺

DAY 13, EARLY MORNING
MAYUR VIHAR, NEW DELHI

"All set?" the man asked Trisha, as if they were friends since forever.

She pursed her lips. Half an hour after he had tied her hands and gagged her, the man had come back, to her surprise, with food and water. He had let her eat the sandwiches and then left her bound and gagged for the rest of the night. Her whole body was aching, and her head throbbed due to lack of sleep.

"Here is your bag and car keys. You reach this point on Highway 44 and stop the car. A man will come to you and tamper with your engine. Then the field is all yours."

"Who is he though?" she asked, banking on her luck.

"He is a very dangerous man, not to be crossed, so be on guard all the time."

"Is he in your gang?"

The man smiled, or it looked like he smiled behind the mask. "You are asking too many questions, Trisha. Yes, he was in our gang."

"What if he doesn't come?" She hoped he did not.

"He will."

She stared at him—a little emboldened to realize that she was an important player in whatever game he was playing. He still hadn't told her anything about Armaan though.

"If not, we abort. We'll bring you back here and no harm will come to your brother. But if you go to the police, we will hunt down your brother and kill him, but will leave you alive and make you suffer." He pulled her hair, causing her eyes to water from the pain. "Don't think you are in charge here, Doc. Don't forget, we'll have eyes and ears on you 24X7. Wear these." He held out a locket, a smart watch and an old model of cell phone.

"What are these?"

"Tracking devices. You are not supposed to take them off yourself at all. If you switch them off, your brother dies. If you take them off, your brother dies. If you call someone other than us, your brother—" He mimed cutting his throat. "If Armaan asks you to call anyone, you will call me on the number fed in the phone and pretend to have a conversation. If he comes to know about anything happening here, your—"

"I know, my brother dies."

⊷⋘◉⋙⊶

CHAPTER EIGHT

Armaan had started early to avoid the office rush hour in Delhi and Gurugram. His route was all mapped out. His first stop was Chandigarh, the planned cosmopolitan city 550kms from the national capital, then to the hills— to cold weather and bliss.

On NH 44, as he crossed Kurukshetra, he saw a crowd on the highway that suddenly dispersed when a figure lashed out waving her hands.

A feeling of déjà vu swept over him as he watched the familiar black car parked at the curb and the person bending over the bonnet of the car—the same brown tresses and that familiar lithe body clad today in simple jeans and a pale pink knitted T-shirt tucked into the waist band. Involuntarily, despite the anger beginning to bubble, he slowed down and stopped behind her vehicle.

She looked up—chic and urbane in her brown sunshades, totally in contrast with the rustic surroundings and roadside gawkers. He shouldn't have stopped. There was still time to back and drive on.

Winding down his window, he angled his head and couldn't help but ask, "Need help?" The people around her, who had begun to come closer again, backed away as he stared at them one by one.

He couldn't see her eyes since she was wearing dark shades but her eyebrows narrowed as she straightened and recognition dawned. If she was glad to see him she didn't show but walked toward him with a purpose, drawing his attention to her slim figure. He experienced the familiar tug of attraction, a deep frustration and a sliver of anger, all rolled into one breath. What was wrong with him?

"Hi! Do you know anything about cars? I could use some help. The network is really bad in this wilderness." She stood near his window chewing on her delectable lower lip, looking a little flustered and unsure of his response.

He sighed, opened his door and surprised her as well as himself by asking, "What will I get if I help you?" He could now see her eyes through the brown shades and she did look worried.

Worry replaced incredulous mistrust as she took a step back. "Whatever you ask for."

He raised his eyebrows, a little amused. "Really? That's some offer."

She pursed her lips.

He stepped out of the car and took off his shades, and stared menacingly at the crowd out there to lech after her. "How about telling me the reason for running away, twice?"

"You have taken it on your ego."

"Oh, it's my ego, not your cowardice?!" He stared down at her as the men began to disperse to the other side of the road.

"I never promised you anything." Her chin rose in challenge.

"You don't say—" He let out a frustrated breath and raked his hair with this fingers to get some control over himself. Anger, exasperation and irritation never worked in any situation. When did he allow her to get under his skin, the way she had? Deep inside, so much so that it jarred his senses.

"So, will you help me?" She was pinching her pinkie finger now.

"God help me, yes, I will. And I hope I'll not get categorized as a loony man left loose on the roads as you did in the parking."

"Will not, if you won't act like a man thriving on paranoia."

"I am not thriving on paranoia. A bullet was fired! I got it investigated."

"Did you find the bullet?"

"No, but the cement on the pillar was chipped."

She sighed. "Look I don't have time to argue with you. Will you help me or not? Or should I look for some other option?"

He glared at her, cursing his grandmother's voice nagging him to always help a woman in distress, then headed toward her car.

Trisha let out a long, silent breath of relief behind his back. She somehow knew challenging him would do the trick. She watched him step up to the open bonnet and fiddle with the engine, checking the various things she had no clue about. The hair on his nape curled against the collar of his black polo T-shirt. Thick hair that she had combed with her fingers many a times that night.

Oh God, who was he? He looked so normal. So polite. She could never have guessed him to be associated with the likes of the men in her house, the goons who were holding Tushar and Dada hostage. Strangely, she wasn't scared of him even though if he was a part of their gang. She still wasn't getting any dangerous vibes from him.

As expected, after half-an-hour of trying everything, he gave up. Something was wrong with the engine, he said, and he couldn't do anything about it. The sun was on full blast in the sky and was making it difficult to stand for long in that sweltering heat.

"Where are you heading? I can help tow the car to the nearest garage for repairs."

"Okay. But I don't have a rope or such a thing."

"I have." That said, he tied her car to his own, asked for directions to the nearest mechanic from one of the courteous locals still loitering around her.

<hr>

By the time they reached the car repair center that was twenty miles away, it was past lunchtime. Looking at the dilapidated shack, Armaan hoped she had her expectations in check. It was a small garage with a battered car heart lying open in front. From the looks of it and the dirt on the engine parts, it seemed it couldn't be put together by any mechanic even if one wanted to.

Armaan had his doubts about the ability of anyone in this area who could even diagnose the trouble in a car like hers. He stepped out of his car, crossed his arms and stood leaning against the bonnet.

"Could you please look into my car?" She approached the short, pot-bellied man, reclining on a chair, which had one leg supported by a stack of bricks. "One moment it was running, then it sputtered and stalled. It won't start now."

Armaan tried not to smile at the polite, respectful tone.

The man scratched his head as she spoke, his eyes never went above her chest.

"Excuse me! I'm talking to you." She sharply repeated her request and opened the bonnet.

The man now scratched his groin, running his tongue over his lips. Her neck went red, as she helplessly looked on.

Amusement left Armaan at the crude gesture. He came onto his toes and walked into the garage. "You go and sit in my car." He handed her the keys.

She took the keys, but didn't leave his side. "How can he be such an asshole?" she muttered under her breath— the cuss word totally fit for the uncouth man.

Despite the disgust Armaan felt for the asshole, a smile sneaked on his lips. The anger and cuss word too sounded like a poem from her mouth.

"Repair *hoga ki nahin?*" Armaan asked the man stepping between the two, hiding her from the man's sight.

"*Nahin,* not possible," he replied then mumbled something under his breath.

"That's it!" She fumed. "Couldn't he have given the same answer to me?" She pursed her lips and stomped back to her car and gave the front tire a solid kick. Good that she was wearing boots instead of those dainty heels that had made his imagination run wild that night.

"Call up an authorized service provider to pick up the car. I can give you a ride to the nearest town. Where are you heading?"

"I have to go to my aunt's farmhouse near Kalka. It's around fifteen kms after we cross Chandigarh, but you can drop me in Chandigarh, then I'll make some arrangements or my aunt will send a car in the morning. If that's not a problem."

"Yeah, sure. No problem."

"Thanks."

Once she located and spoke with a towing service agency, Armaan handed the mechanic a two-thousand-rupee note with the promise of another if the car was found in the same condition when the towing team came to take it away. They rolled her car down to the side of the shop and transferred her luggage to the trunk of his car.

"You shouldn't have given him the money," she said locking her car.

"Then nothing would be left of your car in the four hours it will take for the towing guy to arrive."

"I don't have cash on me right now. I'll pay you back once we reach Chandigarh," she said buckling herself in the passenger seat.

"No issues."

He sat in the driver's seat not doing anything.

"What happened?"

"Am I now fit enough to know your name?"

"Trisha."

He shook his head.

"What?"

"Only Trisha?"

"Trisha Mehra. Do I have to give you my whole bio?"

His eyes turned hard. "Don't try your luck too far, Trisha Mehra. Be nice to me. You are at my mercy to bail you out from this godforsaken place."

She just stared ahead pinching her finger again.

It took him ten minutes on the road to cool down, before starting the much-awaited conversation. "Why did you leave the room like that?"

"You are still stuck on that?"

He gave her a steely look before concentrating back on the road. "You left as if... as if..." His knuckles, on the steering wheel, went white. "As if I was some gigolo out there to please you."

"I believe gigolos get paid."

"So that makes it right! Does it?" God, she was headstrong!

"I don't know why you are so angry? It was a one-night stand. We were attracted to each other and took it forward. Excuse me if I don't know the etiquette of that kind of a night, because it was the first time I did it!"

"That's some information, isn't it?! You are not into one night stands so why make that particular night like one?"

"So you want it to be spelled out in black and white?"

"Don't tempt me to wring your neck, Trisha."

She let out a long breath and closed her eyes. "Well. I met you and found you attractive, that's it. I don't want a relationship. Isn't that self-explanatory?"

"No, it's not! It's not self-explanatory! Courtesy demands that you explain yourself, not sneak out like we'd done something sinful. And then you ran off from the parking lot too when I had asked you for a discussion over coffee."

"You didn't ask. You ordered me."

"What was I supposed to do when someone was shooting at us! Send out an e-invitation for a cup of coffee."

"Did you visit a doctor? You are way too thin and your pallor is not healthy too."

Gripping the steering wheel hard, he didn't look at her and concentrated on driving.

"A vacation might do you good," she insisted.

"Don't change the subject."

"God! What do you want me to say?"

"I never pegged you for a wh… for a loose girl."

"Well, maybe I'm one. Get over it."

A group of college students drove by making a huge ruckus and noise, waving at them.

Silence reigned in the car till Trisha's phone rang. "Hi baby!"

He winced at her sugary tone, but Trisha couldn't help it. It was that man calling to let her talk to Tushar. She had to convey to her brother that everything was alright and he would see her soon.

"Careful, Trisha." It was not Tushar but that hateful masked man. "You want him to cooperate with you. Don't antagonize him. I am putting Tushar on the line now."

"Hi sweetheart, did you have dinner? Yes… yes… I will … I don't know baby… I'll call whenever I have reception next, promise… Bye sweetheart… Be good, don't worry, I'll see you soon."

Armaan couldn't control himself and said, "Was he another one of your self explanatory one night stands?"

She sighed. "Yes."

"Don't lie, damnit!"

Tired beyond words, she leaned back in the seat and closed her eyes.

⸺◈⸺

CHAPTER NINE

"If you don't mind can we stop somewhere in Ambala?" Trisha said after half an hour on the road, "I need a bio break."

"Sure." A few minutes later, Armaan spotted a decent looking hotel right as they entered Ambala city. He had to park the car on the side of the road across the hotel since all the parking slots along the road were occupied.

She reached to unbuckle her seat belt, and so did he. Their hands brushed. The same electric sizzle ran through her hand down to her toes. She immediately pulled back from the contact but couldn't get away from his gaze that had her pinned to the seat.

A car honked somewhere in the parking lot, jolting her out of the trance. Nibbling on her lower lip, she straightened quickly, picked up her handbag and got down.

Letting out a breath, Armaan too stepped out of the car without sparing another glance at her and stretched his arms wide trying to take out the kinks from his shoulders. If she didn't want him, it was fine by him.

"Look out!" someone yelled.

He pivoted midway in his stretching routine and heard before he saw a vehicle roar at a distance coming straight at her. One second, she was rummaging in her bag for her phone, while crossing the road and in the next, everyone began to shout, so she stopped right in the middle of the road.

Her handbag and phone slipped down her hand to the road.

"Trisha, move!" Armaan raced toward her.

He covered the last two feet in a jump and pushed her off out of the vehicle's path. Both of them fell on the side of the road colliding with the bevy of trees and stone pavement. She let out a scream, he grunted and moved off her. Armaan had tried hard not to land on her but there was no space. She groaned again.

The fear had given way to anger. "You idiot! What's the problem with you? Why didn't you move?" Biting down the hiss of pain on his hip, Armaan thundered at her side, keeping the still rolling truck in sight.

Tears gathered in her eyes as she doubled up in agony, clutching her left arm with her right. Everyone was running and shouting around them.

"Are you both okay?" someone asked.

She cursed and exhaled. Armaan glanced at her to make sure that she was okay then trained his gaze on the truck, which had gone past them and collided on the side of the road and stopped, thankfully, without harming anyone else.

"Are you alright, Ma'am?" someone asked again crouching beside her.

"We are fine," Armaan told the concerned man, then turned toward her, "You should've moved, there was ample time," he said toning down his voice, a little guilty at his outburst.

"Well, I couldn't?" she snapped too, but her voice came out as a feeble croak. She cleared her throat and winced at the pain. Her left cheek and arm were bleeding. She touched her fingers to her lips, then brought the bloody fingers down.

"Will you be able to get up?" The stranger crouched down trying to assist her. "Easy… This is really unfortunate. I think both of you should go to a doctor. There's a clinic near the bus stand."

"We'll manage." Armaan elbowed the man off and helped Trisha up. She wobbled a bit. He saw that her jeans were torn around the left knee and guessed that she must have been bruised there too.

"I can help." The man held a hand toward Trisha, trying to support her.

"We are alright. You can leave," Armaan's tone took a hard edge.

"But, Sir, your arm is bleeding," the man said.

"Can't you understand English. I said we both are fine and we'll manage."

The man left in a huff.

"Oh God! Manners!" Trisha said between clenched teeth.

⸺⸱⸎⸙⸙⸱⸺

You stay put here. I want to speak with the police," Armaan said after he delivered Trisha to the doctor's clinic, which was, thankfully, in the next cluster of buildings.

"Shouldn't you see the doctor first? The man was right, your arm is bleeding too."

"It's nothing. I want to speak to the police first or the truck driver if he hasn't run away," he repeated and left, oblivious to her gaze following him all the way out and the deep worry in her eyes that had nothing to do with her injuries.

When that man had shown Trisha Armaan's photo, she thought he was a part of their gang. From their acidic tone, it seemed he had betrayed them somehow. But nothing he did match the negative picture they had painted of him in her apartment. He had been nothing but a gentleman with her, right through that night in Delhi till the time he had delivered her to the doctor a minute back. He was a little short-tempered, but nothing out of ordinary.

But then, nowhere it was written that gangsters had to be discourteous to women.

"Ms. Mehra, the doctor will see you now," the nurse called Trisha pulling her out of her reflections.

Trisha blinked back and limped into the doctor's cabin.

⸻

Armaan came back to the clinic with her handbag and phone, which thankfully was intact, when the doctor was binding a crepe bandage on Trisha's left arm. She had a bruise on her temple and her lips were swollen though the bleeding had stopped. The doctor had put her arm in a sling.

"Hope nothing is broken?" Armaan asked the doctor, placing her bag and phone on the table near the door.

"No, thankfully not. Her ankle is sprained and her arm needed a few stitches. Don't put weight on that ankle for at least 24 hours."

"Are you alright?" he asked turning toward her.

She nodded, looking tired and dejected with the foot bandaged and the doctor still working on her arm. She looked a far cry from the picture she had made at the party. Every time he was around her, she got hurt, he thought. He had seen the bruise on her arm when she had entered her car in the parking lot that day too. She hadn't complained though.

Her grunt when the doctor finished bandaging her arm brought him to the present.

"Nothing to worry about. Just a couple of days rest and medication will do the trick. Use the cane for a few days. I need not tell you the usual precautions," the doctor said handing her the prescription.

Armaan frowned at the remark and the camaraderie between the two, as she nodded. Was she really a doctor?

Trisha looked down at her bandaged ankle and the pair of sneakers the doctor had lent to her.

"Here, let me," Armaan sat down at her feet and took off the lace from the left shoe and widened the opening so that she could slip her bandaged foot.

"No, no… I can do it." Mortified, Trisha tried to pull back her leg unsuccessfully.

"There. It's done." He pulled the loosened sneaker over the bandage gently. The nurse handed her a paper bag that contained her boots and a cane.

"And I think I should examine you too." The doctor turned toward Armaan, bringing his own aches and pains at the forefront.

"I'm fine." His arm throbbed and he had taken a painful thump on his hip as well.

"No, you are not. I see a bruise beginning to form here." The doctor touched Armaan's right elbow.

When Armaan was finally and reluctantly patched and bandaged too, Trisha stood up. Then she heaved, bringing her hands to her mouth. Startled, the doctor shoved the waste bin in the room in front of her and held her by her shoulders.

"I don't think we should rule out a concussion," the doctor said, when Trisha was in control and took long steadying breaths. "It'll be better if you get admitted to the hospital nearby. I am on the visiting panel there and will be able to see you, if needed."

"No, no, I think I'm fine now."

"You are getting admitted," Armaan said in a tone that brooked no argument.

"No, I'm not. I have to reach my aunt's place tonight." This couldn't be happening! She had to get Tushar back that evening. She felt moisture gathering behind her eyes.

He picked up her phone from the examination table and held it out to her. "Call her, and tell her you are getting delayed at least by 36 hours. We'll drive from here day after, after breakfast. I'll drop you all the way to your aunt's."

"36 hours?! No way." It felt like she was in a 3D movie, where she was a part of the experience, but had no control over the events, the characters or her own circumstances. She had thought she would reach the farmhouse by night and would be united with Tushar that very day. Thirty-six hours meant one day and two full nights. How was Tushar going to handle it? He would be scarred for life. She wouldn't be able to endure it either. Oh God! Why?

"You are not in a position to decide. I'm not taking the risk to drive you in this condition."

"I can take a taxi," she blurted, then realized her mistake. Would they be really listening to everything? She glanced at the watch on her wrist.

"Try hiring one." Armaan's lips curled and eyes took a hard glint.

She stared at him, suddenly scared of him. The man who held Tushar as hostage had told her that Armaan was a dangerous man. And the determined expression on his face right now indicated that he was not used to being disobeyed. She took the phone from him and dialed the number Tushar's kidnapper had given her.

The phone connected in two rings. "Hi, Trisha," the man on the other side said.

"Hi, Aunty, how are you? There is a problem. I'm going to be delayed by a couple of days… I've… I've met with an accident here in Ambala…"

"Why did you say that you'll take a taxi?" the man asked.

"No, no, I'm fine. Nothing serious. But the doctor thinks I should stay under observation in a hospital nearby…" Trisha said, trying to breathe normally.

"Never, ever pull that kind of stunt. Remember your brother's innocent face the next time you try something foolish."

"Yes… I do… But what to do. Yes, yes… Don't worry at all. No, I'm not alone. I have a friend traveling with me… Yes, yes."

"Go ahead. You can stay there, but keep him with you. Good job, doctor. You should have been an actor." The man disconnected the call.

"Okay, bye." Trisha spoke into the silent phone and pretended to end the call.

"Staying at a motel is also fine if you don't want to go to a hospital, provided someone is there to watch over you." The doctor sensed her distressful silence as reluctance to get admitted to the hospital and glanced at Armaan. "It's only for the next twenty-four hours."

CHAPTER TEN

Surprised when they reached a hotel, Trisha blurted, "This is not a hospital."

"Good you noticed. It means your brain is still functioning fine." He eased into the hotel's foyer and took out their bags from his car. He held the bags in one hand and with the other, he took her elbow.

"Why are we here?" She masked the hurt at his sarcasm under the pretense of collecting her things. What had she expected? That her injuries and pain would make him polite and compassionate? Why was she even expecting anything from him? He was the reason she was in this nightmare.

All her optimism to meet Tushar by the end of the day had fizzled out. The energy that she had felt in the morning when she had started her car had turned into hopelessness by evening. How was she going to go through two nights and a full day? What if Dada was seriously hurt? What if he did not get medical assistance in time and things got complicated? He was her only link and support in the mission she had set out for herself.

He opened the passenger door and held out his hand.

"I can walk." She managed to get out without taking his hand.

"Didn't know that my touch has suddenly become so abhorrent," he snapped and walked ahead toward the reception desk. By the time she reached him, he had checked them in and was asking for her identification document. She handed over her driving license and looked around. It was quite a good hotel, probably one of the best ones in Ambala.

"The restaurant is down the corridor to the left if you want dinner," the receptionist informed him handing him the keys and the documents.

"We'll order room service. Hope it's available."

"Yes, of course, Sir. Enjoy your stay."

He nodded and took her elbow, and guided her toward the elevators. Suddenly deeply tired of everything, she didn't protest.

"This is it," he said when they entered the room.

She exhaled and rubbed her arms despite the ambient temperature in the room and frowned when he dropped his bag too beside hers. "What's your bag doing in my room?"

"We are sharing a room."

"We are what?"

"I'm staying in this room."

"You are?"

He pulled the door closed, then crossed the room and peered out of the French windows scoping the hotel.

"You don't have to feel responsible or play nursemaid to me. I can hire a nurse. You can take another room."

"Why? Don't tell me you are suddenly shy of me. Remember, I have seen it all."

"What will people think if we share a room?"

"Are you answerable to anyone?"

"No."

"Good. Neither am I. And don't worry I'll take the couch."

She sat down on the bed. The strain of the entire weekend, worry about Tushar and acting as if everything was normal was getting to her. She hadn't slept for two nights in a row. Closing her eyes, she flopped down on the bed.

"What happened? Are you feeling faint? The doctor said—"

She opened her eyes and found him on his knees beside the bed, looming over her. His lovely, worried gaze scanned her face. How could he go from being a scoundrel to irritable to a caring person in seconds? Would they murder him when they reached the farmhouse? Would it be justified? He could be innocent. For all she knew maybe the goon in her apartment could be lying. Oh God! What mess has she landed into?

"Trisha?"

"I'm fine," she snapped, totally on edge. "Just tired. And you can shed this caring facade, no one is here to watch you." She hated the whining tone her voice had taken.

He scanned her face for a few seconds, then eased off, apparently satisfied. "I think you should eat something. We missed lunch too."

"I don't want anything. I just want to sleep." To her chagrin, she felt a hot lava of tears behind her eyelids at the concern and sympathy in his tone.

"We'll see. Why don't you change and settle down?" Armaan suggested after he had checked the bathroom. "I'll order dinner. What do you want?"

"Nothing. I don't feel like eating." It won't do to cry in front of him, so she got up, pulled out a hand towel from her overnight bag, summoned all her energy and hopped to the bathroom.

"Don't lock the door." A little worried, Armaan watched her as she hobbled into the bathroom. Something seemed off.

By the time she came out, he had finished checking each and every corner of the room, including the closet and the balcony, and had also ordered dinner.

She sat on the bed in a red, polka-dot, flannel pajamas, applying an ointment on her bruises, looking nothing like a doctor or a surgeon. The desire to have a normal, civilized conversation with her overwhelmed him so much that he stepped back into the balcony. It was becoming difficult to remain angry or to keep his distance.

The room bell rang indicating their dinner had arrived.

She kept her eyes averted when the waiter came in with their food. Her sudden shyness after that night of inhibited passion told him volumes about her behavior. She looked so vulnerable and dejected that the sting of her sneaking out after that night was diminishing with every passing minute.

He forked a little pasta and chicken salad on a plate, and took it to her. "I didn't know what you liked. But those medicines shouldn't be taken on an empty stomach.

Doctor's words." He smiled in truce, but his smile was wasted.

She took the plate without lifting her eyes. Her silent, resigned expression had guilt rising within him. Perhaps he had been too harsh with her, more so after the accident. Her phone rang, loudly dissecting the silence of the room, startling both of them.

She placed the plate on the side table and picked up the phone. "Hi, Tush, how are you? Did you eat something?" She bit her trembling lower lip and dry swallowed.

Armaan tried not to stare or frown at the emotions swirling on her face and the effort she exerted to control herself. This was no friend or a boyfriend.

" … … Speak to me baby, please. I'm so sorry… … I'll be back soon. I have some work here… Yes, yes, surgery. As soon as the patient is stable, I'll be home soon." She then looked at the ceiling and blinked fast. "You have dinner. Dada is at home, don't worry. I'll come home soon. Bye, sweetheart." She sniffled as she put the phone down.

When a drop of water plonked down on her hand and she covered her eyes with her palm, he realized she was crying. Every ounce of anger and irritation drained out of him.

"Trisha?" He placed his plate back on the coffee table, and took her in his arms. To his shock, hiding her face in her hands, she broke down into loud sobs. "What happened? Who was that?" She didn't say anything, just kept crying. What did you do when a woman cried the way she was right now? It was sheer torture, and he didn't have a clue on how to handle the situation.

"Is everything okay back home?" he asked when the sobs were replaced by light hiccups. She pushed at his chest, so he released her.

She sat back and rummaged into her purse, pulling out a pack of tissues.

"Um… Is it hurting too much? I think you can take your painkillers with the food," Armaan tried again.

She took a deep breath and took her medicine from the medicine foil. After having a few spoons of salad and the medicine, she meekly slid inside the comforter and closed her eyes.

Armaan glanced at the side table beside the bed. Who was that on the phone? Looking at her distress, he didn't press her, but it seemed like she was talking to a child. Armaan guessed it was the same kid she'd spoken to on the way to Ambala too. And she had lied over the phone pretending that she was in the hospital. Did she have an offspring? Was she married? She had said she wasn't answerable to any one. Divorced? He glanced at her again. Her smooth, slow breathing indicated she had slipped into deep sleep.

There was something amiss but he was unable to put a finger to it. His observation skills had gone completely haywire as far as she was concerned. That night at the party she was relaxed, but today, she seemed totally high-strung. What could be the reason? Was her aunt not well? He ran his fingers through his hair for the umpteenth time to bring in objectivity and focus, but couldn't.

⸻⸻◈◈◈⸻⸻

Try as he might, Armaan was unable to sleep on the narrow couch. He should have asked for another bed, he thought, as he eyed the space on the bed beside Trisha. His arm and hip still throbbed in pain and he was unable to sleep on his left side. He picked up his phone and looked at the time. It was not even midnight. The day was just not ending.

He got up resignedly, wore his jacket and went to the window. He parted the blinds a bit and was on full alert in seconds. It was a starry night and the parking lot was visible under the golden glow of the wrought iron lamp posts. A car was parked in the parking lot of the hotel and the red glow of a cigarette, dangling out of the partially rolled down window. The man inside took a drag, brought his hand out of the window, and tapped a finger on the cigarette butt dropping the ash down on the ground.

Armaan wished he had a pair of binoculars on him.

He let the blind fall back and looked at Trisha. She was sleeping on her side with her face toward him. He frowned and wondered about their chance meetings. She hadn't taken off her smart watch. Nothing abnormal. People did sleep with it to monitor their sleep pattern and heart rate.

Still, he couldn't ignore his instincts.

He got up and checked her phone. It was an old model and had a screen password. Nothing new, since most people kept their phones password protected. He unzipped her overnight bag and searched it, then searched her handbag too. He found nothing out of ordinary.

Was he actually suffering from PTSD—suspecting everything and everyone?

Armaan couldn't help but wonder who could be sitting in the car in the parking lot so late in the night. He could be someone's driver who didn't get a room in the hotel or one with stingy owners who didn't want to pay for the driver's comfort, he tried to tell himself. Could it be that innocent an explanation? Armaan held his head as he contradicted his own thoughts and ideas.

As a deep-ingrained precautionary measure, he sent a text to Karan informing him about the circumstances, his detour to Chandigarh and then his plan to drop Trisha at her aunt's farmhouse on Monday. He could have asked Karan to run an identity check on Trisha, but that would have been an invasion of her privacy and would not sit well if she came to know, more so when he was thinking of courting her when they were back in Delhi.

Everything that had happened was normal, even though it didn't feel normal to him. Maybe he really needed a few sessions with Doc.

After a few more minutes of struggling to find a comfortable position on the couch, he gave up and made a beeline for the bed.

⎯⎯◦❈◦❈◦⎯⎯

DAY 14, MID-MORNING
AMBALA, HARYANA

Armaan stirred, stretched, and his heart thudded when something blocked his arm. He couldn't move it. Alarmed, his eyes snapped open and saw Trisha, deep in sleep, cuddled against him. Shifting to the bed had been a decision he was now pleased about.

Pleased with the situation, he relaxed and watched her. She was facing him, her head resting on his arm and hand on his stomach. Memories came rushing and his heartbeat accelerated again. This was how he had wanted her that morning after the wedding reception, minus the bruises, of course. Her long lashes touched her cheeks and her lips. Her thigh flush against his own stirred another wave of emotions within… He let out a long, silent breath.

He had never been so attracted to the opposite sex as he was to her. The urge to be with her and protect her had surpassed anything he had ever experienced before. And that night…

To take his mind off his lusty thoughts, he scanned her and took stock of her injuries. The bruise on her lips was healing well. The bandage on her elbow had loosened and he could see it was going to give her some trouble, as would her internal injuries.

What started out as an unconscious comfort seeking need that night in Delhi had changed into deep attraction, with affection thrown into the mix—at least for him. The urge to take care of her was so strong that it had blocked all rational thoughts from his mind. It was entirely his own fault that he was now committed to deliver her to her aunt in one piece.

She stirred and groaned softly. He closed his eyes.

⸻⸱❖⸱⸻

CHAPTER ELEVEN

The mattress dipped on Trisha's side and Armaan forced himself to relax. He could feel her eyes skimming his face. The thought that she could see his body's reaction to her presence made it both pleasant and uncomfortable. He tried to suppress the sensation and ignore the discomfort and lay still.

Gauging her thoughts and emotions toward himself was like watching a swinging pendulum. Sometimes, he felt she was interested and at times she would go into a shell, which, given the newness of their association he didn't feel that he had the right to breach at the moment.

When her breath fanned his lips, he couldn't control himself and caught hold of her wrist lying on his stomach.

She gasped and shrank into her pillow pulling her hand back. "Oh… I thought… sorry."

He blinked as if coming out of deep sleep. "Hey."

"I guess the couch wasn't comfortable enough," she said.

"Yeah. Did you sleep well?"

"Good enough, given the circumstances."

Her swollen eyes reminded him of her distress last night and a wave of sympathy rolled into his chest. "So, tell me, what's your name?"

She frowned and stared at him as if he had lost his marbles.

"It's a test." He held up his hand. "How many fingers do you see?" When she didn't say anything, he added, "Just checking if the upper story is intact." He smiled and tapped her temple, but didn't get an answering smile.

She looked at him solemnly, got up with a jerk, then hissed and groaned, and flopped back on the bed.

"You should take it slow," he said. When she still didn't respond, he continued, "Shall we call for a truce, Trisha? Please."

For a moment, it seemed she wasn't going to answer, but then she closed her eyes and sighed. "Okay."

"Is it hurting a lot?"

"Yes, some."

She opened her mouth to say something then changed her mind. "I think I should get up and see if all my bones and joints are intact or not."

"What is troubling you, Trisha? You know you can tell me."

No answer.

He too sighed and got up. "Let me call room service for breakfast, so you can take your medicines. What do you prefer?"

Trisha picked up her vanity bag and hurried to the bathroom. "Anything is fine." Tears made their presence felt again at his sympathy and concern. It was better when he was prickly and sarcastic. God! What did she want?

When she came back, the breakfast was on the coffee table. She had composed herself and had even put on some eye makeup to conceal the telltale signs of tears.

"Come and have something before taking your medicines." He sat down after freshening up and tried to conceal his own wince from the pain. Now that the injury had cooled down, his hip must be making the discomfort known.

"I'm sorry. You are hurt because of me," she said when he handed her a plate of steaming *idlis* and *sambhar*. "Don't know what happened to me on the road. One minute I was okay and the next I couldn't even feel my feet beneath."

He studied her for a moment, then brought his attention back to his plate, apparently satisfied with the examination. "Never mind."

"Still, thank you for saving my life." She watched him serve himself. His damp hair stuck to his skull and curled over the collar of his grey T-shirt. It had been ten days since the party. Though he was still lean, he looked much better—rested and relaxed.

He nodded, his focus on his plate and the breakfast. "I'll not say you're welcome." He smiled and looked up.

Caught staring, she dropped her eyes to her plate. A faint flush rose from her neck to her ears. She began to push around the tiny pieces of *idli* on her plate. "What happened to the truck driver?" she asked flicking a glance at him.

Amused, he continued to look at her, so she picked up a spoonful of her breakfast and put it in her mouth.

"Did he run away?"

"No." To her relief, he resumed eating as he replied, "According to the driver, the truck's brakes malfunctioned. This particular make of trucks do not have a hand brake and I think the driver was drunk. Suicidal idiot." He told her about his interaction with the driver, and the fact he wasn't convinced with the explanation the man had given him. In the few seconds that he had watched the truck, it was right in the center of the road before suddenly veering toward Trisha. Armaan was sure that the man was drinking and driving.

"Is he alright though?" She added half a spoon of *sambhar* into the already filled bowl.

"You know you can look at me. I won't mind."

"What?" Her eyes jerked to his face.

"I know I'm quite good looking and I don't mind pretty ladies admiring me."

"Really?" Amusement steamrolled over shyness as she sat back crossing her arms.

"Yeah." He smiled and reached for another *idli* when she declined a second serving. "I… er… I'm sorry, but are you really a doctor? I had some other impression."

"What impression did you have?"

"At the party I thought you were… a companion, an arm candy, as they say… that was because of Gaekwad. He carries the reputation of a Casanova…"

"Does he?"

"…and you are pretty attractive." He looked into her eyes before his gaze went straight to her lips.

The air went thick with undercurrents again. Her heart thudded pleasantly and her body tightened. She looked away and tried to lighten the mood. "So you classified me into a pre-defined category? How typical!"

"Oh, it was just an innocent conclusion. And it was reinforced when you sneaked out of the hotel room."

"Are you ever going to stop mentioning that night?"

"Not till the time I know the real reason for you leaving the way you did."

"It felt all right that night, but in broad daylight it was different."

"How? What had changed?"

She became uncomfortable and picked up the medicine foil. "Okay. It was a bad idea to begin with."

"It wasn't!"

Her face went hot again, and she dropped her gaze to the medicine strip in her hand. "I'm not looking for a relationship."

"Why not?"

"It's complicated."

"You know, you don't fit the image of a dedicated doctor." He changed the subject.

"Really? What do I look like?"

"A model perhaps or a page 3 celebrity."

She snorted.

"What's your specialization?"

"Trauma Surgery."

"Wow… Did you start medical education from kindergarten? How old are you?"

She raised her eyes to him then narrowed them. "It's not polite to ask that. For all you know, I might be older than you."

"Impossible. I'll be twenty-nine in August."

She began to smile and then winced in pain.

"Don't tell me…" He shook his head.

"I have to tell you…two months. I'm older than you by two months." She wiggled two fingers.

"Unbelievable… Did you get a plastic surgery done?" Frowning mischievously, he held her chin and peered closely.

"Don't be silly." She tugged her chin free, suddenly shy, and dropped her gaze to her phone again.

"It's really an ugly phone."

"Yeah, so it is. My phone fell down and was damaged, so I am making do with this old model. Didn't have time to buy a new one. Someone lent this to me since I was in a hurry."

Too much explanation, he began to think then clamped down on his detective mode. "It's okay. You don't have to justify using an old phone, lot's of people do. So tell me about your aunt's place."

"Er… It's a farmhouse and we loved spending our summer vacations there."

"We?"

"My brother and I."

"Younger or older?"

"Younger." She smiled with affection, then winced again.

"So what should we do today?"

"What can we do when the only playing ground is this room and…" She stopped and flushed pink when he looked at the bed.

"Not a bad idea," he said grinning.

"No, no, I meant—"

"I know. Relax. And I have another great idea." He stood up. "Be back in half an hour."

—————◦❈◦❈◦❈◦—————

DAY 14, EVENING
AMBALA, HARYANA

"You are not sneaking on this bed again tonight. The couch it is for you, Mr. Armaan, don't push your luck like yesterday." Trisha's mood picked up with every passing hour.

To pass the time Armaan had picked up all kinds of board games he could find in the local market. It had been a fantastic idea. They had just played a second round of Scrabble, and she had won again. The thought of having to wait for just one more night before she'd finally be able to meet Tushar made her feel better than she had the day before.

"Afraid that you won't be able to control your urges around me, Doc?"

"Talk about yourself, mister." As the day progressed, it was getting easier to smile.

"Oh... I'm oblivious to your charms," he replied grinning.

"Anyway, it's settled, you are asking for another room or sleeping on the couch. Twenty-four hours of waiting over me will get over in two hours' time." Her phone rang before he could give a befitting reply.

"Hi sweetheart... I called you in the morning but you were sleeping... Yes, I told you..." She got up and moved to the window, "I'm going to Aunt's... Yes, yes... Sure thing. Next time we will take a vacation together darling... Yes of course. I love you too... Bye... Be good."

She kept the phone down and turned to find him glaring at the game board. She took a deep breath. "That was my younger brother on the phone. He is a... ummm... a special needs boy. A teenager though. He had an accident when he was seven."

"Is it because of him you don't want to have a life of your own?"

Uncomfortable discussing her personal circumstances, she rubbed her brows, then said, "Look Armaan, I can't make friends easily. I—"

"We are beyond friendship, sweetheart."

Color rose from her neck to her cheeks. "Please. I can't let anyone in my life right now."

"Why not?"

"I can't."

He took his time to digest the ridiculous reason for the rejection, then left her to pace the small room. "How old is your brother?"

"Seventeen."

The room bell rang and a waiter wheeled the dinner trolley in.

"We can't possibly eat so much," she said, when she saw the number of dishes on it.

"You should. You are way too thin."

"What has happened to you?" she said trying to capture their earlier light mood, "First you categorized me as a… what was that repulsive term you had used?"

"Companion. Arm candy," he supplied.

"Yes, arm candy. Then you whacked me in your attempt to save me, and now you are going to torment me through food and drink?"

He shook his head, a bit annoyed. He didn't want the playful exchange of words. He wanted her trust. He wanted her to confide in him. "I'm glad I can amuse you."

If she noticed his curt tone, she didn't let it on. They had their dinner in uncomfortable silence.

She placed her empty plate on the table and sighed, stretching her back slowly, testing her muscles, then winced. "I think I'll call it a day," she said and picked up her vanity bag, then headed toward the bathroom.

Armaan realized he'd have to settle for a cold shower that night too.

⸻⸻

That night too, Armaan kept an eye on the parking lot but the van wasn't there. He let the blinds fall back, when he heard her stirring and found her reaching out for the water bottle on the side table. They had kept the bathroom lights on for the night. Soft light falling in the room made her look all the more fragile.

"Unable to sleep?" He sat down on one of the low chairs beside the bed.

"Yeah."

"You can have another painkiller. It has been six hours since you took the last one."

She nodded.

"I'm sorry I couldn't control my flight and landed on you quite heavily," he said looking at her.

"Please don't make me laugh." She raised her hand to her lips to control her smile.

Bemused, he raised his eyebrows.

"You are serious! Really? Can you control yourself while moving like that?" she asked, eyes big on her face.

"Yes, of course. You have to take traction from somewhere and roll off. I couldn't because there was no space."

Somehow, she found his explanation amusing. Trisha smiled then winced as she held her lower lip to prevent the skin from stretching. "Then I won't accept your apology. My back is hurting like hell." She bit her cheek.

He nodded and stared at her, his eyes all soft and solemn. All the oxygen in the room got sucked up as they looked at each other. She blinked and stared down at the water bottle she held. He got up and sat beside her, and before she could react Armaan held her face in his hands and kissed her swiftly and thoroughly.

"We really shouldn't," she whispered putting her fingers on his lips.

Armaan tightened his arms around her and bit her lower lip. Something he'd been dying to do it for a long time. "You drive me crazy with your come hither and get lost looks."

"I'm doing nothing of that sort!" Trisha looked on, her eyes wide when he got up and lay down on the other side of the bed.

He could hear incredulity in her tone in the dark. "Good night, doc."

"I knew you won't be able to control your urges around me," she said.

"You were right." He smiled.

"What about my urges?" she asked in a soft tone, throwing all caution to the wind. This was a man who could be... no... who was a gangster. He belonged to a gang that was murderously seeking him out. Because of him her brother's life was in danger and she in this situation. Yet. Yet she wanted his lips on her. She wanted his hands kneading her body as he had done that night. And what if he was innocent?

"I'm sure you have a handle on them."

"What if I don't?" she said and leaned over him. Her hands on his chest, she could feel his heart beating in the same rhythm as hers.

He looked at her, so serious, and sexy.

She leaned toward him, traced his jaw bone with her finger, and put her lips on him. After a few seconds he held both her arms and pulled her gently on top of him, blanket and all. She traced his lips with her tongue, laced her fingers in his hair and pulled his mouth closer, both their breaths mingling and their hearts beating as one.

Armaan's hands stroked her back and waist. He wanted to put his hands inside her pajama top but knew she would put the invisible barrier up if he became a dominant partner. He had to take it slow, convince her that he was up for a long haul.

"Trisha…" he mumbled against her lips when it became too passionate and all he wanted to do was tear their clothes apart and bury himself deep inside her.

"Yeah… What?" Eyes closed, she lifted her mouth fractionally. Panting and embarrassed, she turned away from him to her side of the bed.

He smiled and lay thinking about the spontaneous combustion people claimed, a theory he had never believed. But now that he had experienced it first hand it was hard to deny it. No matter how much she resisted he had to explore to see where their attraction took them. He couldn't just let go of what they had between them. It was definitely not going to be a one or two night stand.

Sleep was hard to come. He heard her deep breaths for a very long time before sleep took hold of him.

CHAPTER TWELVE

Mahi was worried.

Trisha had never missed her weekly morning run in the past two years since Trisha had shifted to this apartment. Mahi had even texted her to remind her but there was no response.

Over the weekend, Mahi had been to her mother's so she'd missed meeting the sister and brother for the past two days. It was a Monday morning and she hadn't even heard Tushar leaving for the school. Was Trisha not well? That could be the only reason for missing her workout.

After Nikhil left for his office, Mahi marched down to Trisha's apartment and rang the bell. There was no response. She could swear someone peeped through the door, but no one opened the door or called out from inside. She waited for Trisha to reply to her text till ten a.m. in the morning, then called up her hospital. "Dr. Trisha Mehra's brother is not well and she is on leave."

⸻⟐⸻

"What should I order for breakfast?" Armaan asked when she came out of the bathroom, all ready to leave.

The dark shadows were back on her face. He had found her sitting in the balcony, lost in her thoughts when he had woken up.

"Can we have it en route? I'm tired of eating here and staring at the walls of this room."

"Yes, of course. In fact, that's a good idea." He called up the hotel reception and informed them that they would like to checkout.

"I'll pay."

"No way. It was my decision."

"It was my accident."

He pursed his lips and stared at her.

"We'll split," she amended her offer when she realized the idiocy of her argument.

"Of course. No two ways about it. Fifty-fifty it is." He smiled.

She gave an answering one, but the smile didn't reach her eyes.

Armaan couldn't understand her sudden reticence and almost unfriendly behavior. It seemed last night was a dream. She went about her business and got ready without meeting his eyes. He couldn't put his finger on the issue but they were back to square one. Again.

"You know you can share your problems with me, Trisha."

Trisha looked at the phone then back at him. "Problem?" She shrugged. "There is no problem, none at all."

He sighed. "Okay, if you say so." They hadn't even exchanged phone numbers. He'd ask her when they reached her aunt's. "Ready?" he asked, zipping his bag closed.

"Yeah." She nodded, throwing another weak, pretend smile at him.

The first leg of the drive was spent with him perpetually glancing in the rear-view and side-view mirrors, looking out for a tail. Half an hour later, he relaxed when no one seemed to be following them.

After a while, Armaan felt Trisha lean against the seat. He looked at her. She was asleep. She had had an uncomfortable night, moaning a few times when she had turned in her sleep. He parked the car to the side and slowly eased the lever of the passenger so that she was in a reclining, comfortable position. She let out a faint sigh. Looked like the painkillers she had taken after her morning tea were working their magic.

He couldn't help but admire her sharp slightly upturned nose and that sexy protruding lower lip. He had to acknowledge he was turning green whenever he thought about her and without him or with someone else. He would have to think of a way to stay with her. Maybe he could charm her aunt and wrangle an invitation to stay there.

She looked so fragile. He had a sudden urge to shield and protect her. From what? He didn't know. He had his doubts that he didn't voice in front of her. She would just mock him as she had done in the parking lot. He had a dreadful premonition that this trip was turning into work.

It was raining when they reached Chandigarh. Armaan smelled the wet pine trees and savored the moment. The panoramic view of the mountains was breathtaking. They reached Chandigarh too soon for his liking.

As he parked the car near a restaurant, he glanced at his passenger, who was sprawled on the adjacent seat oblivious to the world. A copper lock of her hair hid one of her eyes and her face rested on the seat pushing her cheek, making her lips pout a little. He wanted to plant a kiss on the pale pink lips, but he refrained from indulging.

"Trisha…" He touched her cheek, and on a crazy impulse traced her lower lip with his thumb, but the disturbance didn't register.

She had had a rough night. The reclining position probably was comfortable. Sleep might help her heal faster, so he sat in the car watching the passersby, waiting for her to wake up on her own.

Trisha stirred about half an hour later. Armaan looked at her eyelashes fluttering and her tongue tracing the lower lip, which was probably a bit dry given that she was sleeping with her mouth open. He smiled as her eyes opened with a start. Her eyes were still dazed from the remnants of her sleep. "What happened?" she whispered.

"Wanted to kiss the sleeping beauty, but I am no prince," he whispered too as his eyes dropped to her lips.

Her eyes widened, as a pink blush spread all over her face. "Oh, my God!" She sat up with a jerk, so quickly that it was comical. The phone in her lap slid down to the floor of the car. "Have we reached? Why didn't you wake me up?"

"Relax, it's okay."

"You should have woken me up… What's the time?" she asked as she straightened the seat.

"11:55 a.m."

"I was suffering from mild insomnia and now I seem not to get enough of it."

"Why weren't you able to sleep?" he asked, trying to gather as many crumbs about her life he could, like a pathetic, love-struck teenager. Love? Really! Where did that come from?

"It was very hectic and stressful, you know how it is," she was saying, "…one gets sucked up into their daily routine, everything seems more important than the other and you can't leave out anything or anyone except yourself," she said straightening up and adjusted her sling. "What's this place?"

"A little *dhaba*, I had visited once. The food is great and the place is clean and hygienic. Thought we should have brunch here, then be on our way."

"Okay." She nodded, then bit her lip again.

Noticing her worry, another possibility occurred to him. "Are you afraid that your aunt will get scandalized if she sees me, a stranger, with you?"

Her phone vibrated, that same number flashing on the screen. He had memorized that number.

"I guess not." She chewed her lips and made no attempt to take the call.

"Then that's one concern out of the way."

She didn't say anything, her eyes had a moist sheen now.

"Trisha, why are you so worried?"

"No, I'm not." She blinked then gave him a fake, bright smile. "Not worried at all. In fact, I'm starving. Let's go." Not meeting his eyes, she replied, "I hope you are right about the food here."

"You bet." He wasn't fooled by her false chatter but he took it in his stride and stepped out of the car, walking around to the passenger side to help her out. "Don't forget the cane."

Brunch was a simple and silent affair.

Trisha's mood was progressively spiraling down as they neared the end of the meal. The guilt of leading Armaan to a trap, if he was innocent, and worry for her brother were eating her alive. Her phone pinged. She looked at the incoming text and stared, then sighed.

"Shall we?" he asked after asking for the check from the waiter.

"I need to go to the washroom. Be back soon." She stood up, hanging her handbag on her shoulder, and picked up her cane.

"Yeah, sure. Take your time. I'll wait outside."

Trisha entered the bathroom and her phone pinged again. Her heart began to hammer as she followed the instruction and went into the last cubicle. Lifting the lid from the plastic flush, she peered inside and saw the package taped to the side of the water tank.

***

DAY 15, AFTERNOON
EN ROUTE FARMHOUSE

Okay, I see the *mandir*. You are supposed to guide me now."

Trisha wrung the tissue in her hand and nodded. "Armaan…"

"Yeah?" he answered absentmindedly, trying to avoid the potholes that were filled with rain water. It was getting increasingly difficult to estimate the depth. "You were saying something?"

Her phone pinged again.

"Who is texting you so doggedly?"

"No one important. Okay, turn right."

They reached the quaint little place passing a cluster of huts surrounded by yellow mustard fields. He saw the house and was impressed. It was a colonial era bungalow with a stone facade with bougainvillea climbing on the pillars.

"Quite impressive." He looked around stopping at the gate. "And quite deserted. Are you sure this is the right place?"

"Yeah." Trisha hobbled out of the car, clutching her handbag.

He too stepped out and stared at the massive property as they walked toward the gate. "Do they have an electronic bell or do we have to pull some string to ring the bell?" He peered at the empty guard house, then looked over his shoulder at Trisha. Moving like an automaton, he turned slowly as all the warmth in his eyes melted away.

"Armaan, I'm really sorry. I didn't have a choice!" she whispered, aiming the gun at his chest.

CHAPTER THIRTEEN

For a second, Armaan couldn't move. Then something clicked in place—her hesitant answers, the unexplained silences and her vacillating reactions throughout the trip. "I was wondering when this farce was going to end and how. Though I am shocked, but I'll admit that I'd thought of this scenario too. Unfortunately, I dismissed it too early." His eyes turned hard and cold as Trisha's became moist. "So, you are now going to shoot me? Are you Trisha?" He stepped forward. "You could have killed me any time since yesterday, but you didn't. Why?" He took one more step. "Why now?"

"Stay right where you are, please Armaan." She backed one step.

"Oh yeah?" He took another step toward her. "Or what? You'll press the trigger?" He kept going, when he saw that her hand holding the gun was trembling. "Come on, one press of a finger and I'll be gone. Is that what you want?" He stopped when the nozzle was flush against his chest. "Or have they ordered you to just restrain me? I wonder who they are?"

"You knew?"

"Do you think a rookie like you can take me for a ride? When did they give you the gun? It wasn't there last night when I searched your things."

"You searched my things?"

"Who are you working for?" He took out his own gun but held it down. He realized that she hadn't protested when she saw him taking out the gun and filed the information in the corner of his mind.

She looked all around, probably waiting for the cavalry.

"Don't try anything funny, Trisha. You might not know but I am pretty fast and have a deadly aim. Who are you working for?"

"Oh, she won't shoot, but my men will."

It was an effort to feign indifference and surprise when Armaan's eyes landed on the man walking on the driveway across the gate. Smug and smiling, waving a gun. So this was what it was all about? Danish had tracked him down and used Trisha, if that was her actual name, to lure him here. Behind him were two more men wearing a mask.

"One misstep and my men will shoot you down," Danish shouted again and pointed a finger at another masked man on the roof, who had a sniper rifle aimed at Armaan. "Drop the gun and put your hands up. Hands on your head, Sameer."

"Who are you?" Armaan narrowed his eyes.

"Put the gun on the ground, slowly!" Danish barked, "I have three men with their guns trained at you, Sameer. They will kill you like a street dog if you don't do as I say. Just bend and keep the gun on the floor. Real slowly."

"Are you talking to me?" Armaan scowled, but put the gun down. "I think you've got the wrong person. My name is not Sameer. It's Armaan."

"Sameer, Armaan what is the difference, buddy? What matters is what you did. And you have done enough damage. I know all about you. So, you tell me, what do you prefer me to call you? Armaan or Sameer?" His men came forward and put handcuffs around Armaan's wrists. "Take him."

Trisha stepped forward. "Where—"

"Silence!" Danish shouted. "Go in the living room and wait for me."

"You have no right—"

He swung his arm and it landed straight on her face. The cane fell from her hands, she toppled back and collided with Armaan. Pain radiated to her brain as her lip split open and began to bleed again. She had to hold on to Armaan's arm, that was locked behind his back, to steady herself.

"Don't mess with me, woman. Do as you are told!" Danish screamed the last sentence and picked up the gun. "Take him away!" They put a blindfold on Armaan's face and pushed him forward.

Trisha tenaciously followed the man, who seemed like a leader and one of the masked men back to the house after the other two had taken Armaan behind the house.

Little did she know that her horror had just started.

DAY 15, AFTERNOON
FARMHOUSE

As Trisha followed the leader, the man who had threatened Armaan, she watched the men around and tried hard to recognize the two who had invaded her home, but couldn't make out who was who. She had seen only one of the men, that too only his dark, black eyes. The man who was with Tushar was a thin guy. The fact that Tushar might be inside made her hurry inside the house.

The sprawling house with carved pillars and marble staircase was dusty and making her nose twitch. Where would they have kept Tushar? She looked around. The ground floor had a grand granite floor lobby with an ornate staircase winding to the upper floors. Was he upstairs somewhere?

"Where is my brother?" she asked but did not get a response. The man just kept walking to a room across the staircase. "Are you the one who sent goons to my home? Why did you do this? Where is my brother?" Trisha asked, stepping forward when he entered what looked like a living room with carved, antique furniture and a stone fireplace.

Cocking his head to one side, the man watched her for a few seconds, making her uncomfortable, while another masked man stood in the corner watching them.

"You are indeed quite beautiful. My men tell me that Sameer slept with you. He never touched a woman when he was with me. I thought he swayed the other way, you know. But naa… now I know better. One more thing added to his list of sins." He went and sat on a sofa as if he was a king. He was a handsome, lanky man with long hair combed back falling on his shoulders.

"Where is my brother?" she asked again.

He grinned like a madman. "You are spirited. So battered and limping, but your spirit is intact. What love can do to you! Ah, will you have some lemonade or perhaps you prefer harder things?"

The innuendo was not lost on her, but there was no point in getting involved. "I want to take my brother home! That day, those men, your men, assured me that I will find him here if I bring Armaan. I have fulfilled my side of the bargain. Now I just want my brother and I'll be on my way." She placed the phone on the table and unstrapped the watch they had given her. "Here are your things." She kept the watch and the locket beside the phone.

"You are not in a position to demand anything, sweetheart."

"They said I'll find my brother here if I did as they said." She scowled. "I did what they told me to. Now I want to see him, meet him now. Where is he? Tell me, or else—"

"Don't threaten me, woman!"

She tried not to step back and took a deep breath. "Where is he?" It was becoming a never-ending nightmare.

"In Delhi."

"What? That man told me he will bring him here!"

"Do you fathom that I would play nanny to a freak?"

"My brother is not a freak, you bastard!"

"Careful, Dr. Mehra. I can't abide by irreverent woman no matter how pretty they are."

"Then drop me to the nearest bus station. I'll go back home and you can instruct your men to leave my brother alone. I give you my word that we will not talk about this whole sordid business to anyone."

The mad man only laughed.

⸻❖❖❖⸻

DAY 15, AFTERNOON
FARMHOUSE

"I'm sorry, Armaan," someone whispered, someone he had trusted.

No, he didn't. Yes, he did…

The argument continued in his mind, but he couldn't recognize the face. The voice faded as the pain in his arm announced its presence. He winced, but couldn't move his arm. It felt as if a boulder was kept on his head. His eyes were still glued together and refused to open. He felt like an old man who couldn't even keep his head upright. Danish's face appeared on the canvas of his brain. How had he tracked him? What had given him away?

Armaan willed his eyes open and found himself in a dark, dingy room. He was sitting in an uncomfortable wrought iron chair with his arms bound at the back. The smell of jungle, damp and must lingered around him making him take shallow breaths. He had no inkling about the time. The room had a window but it was heavily barred with wooden planks. Across the room, near the door, Danish's bodyguard, Shiva, a huge, ugly man, sat on the floor picking his nose and drinking from a bottle, lost in his thoughts. During his stint at Amrtisar with Danish he had interacted with Shiva and Armaan knew he fought ugly when provoked. For the moment Armaan ignored him as he ignored him.

The day's events began to play in fast forward. One moment Armaan was interrogating Trisha and the next, Danish had appeared and apprehended him. He had even backhanded Trisha, when she said something. Something that had angered Danish and he had asked her to keep quiet.

Was she really part of their gang? The whole thing was a charade! Right from the party. Was sleeping with him too a part of the charade? Or was she in some kind of duress? Her tears and emotional see-saw told him that she was an unwilling partner. But then she had ample chances to confide in him during the time they were in the motel. Why hadn't she asked for help? How did she even know Danish? Was she really a doctor?

She had followed Danish inside the house.

They had put a hood on his face, then he had felt a pinch on his arm and had staggered. Someone had supported him and led him to… to where? He didn't remember. Was he in the same property or transported somewhere else? How many hours had he been unconscious?

He knew his questions were not going to be answered till he was out of this godforsaken situation. He had to think of a way to cut loose. With practiced ease, he blanked his mind and felt his limbs and fingers. Nothing was broken, though his arms and feet were numb due to lack of circulation. He twisted his hand, felt the band and found the little blade hidden inside the cuff of his jacket, pressing against his skin. He flicked his wrist and the blade slipped down on his palm. He slowly began to open the hand cuff.

The friction made some noise and Shiva's red eyes turned toward Armaan and glared. Armaan stopped the movement and stared back at him, noting the knife in his boot and the gun in his waistband. Shiva looked at him as if Armaan was a piece of furniture and began to clean his teeth, with the makeshift toothpick.

⸻ ⬦⬦⬦ ⸻

DAY 15. AFTERNOON
ZENITH HOSPITAL. NEW DELHI

"Ms. Paul tells me Trisha is not in today?" Priya asked Udit, taking off the cap of her OT scrubs.

"Is it?" Udit asked looking at his gorgeous partner in front of him and thanking the Almighty for her presence in his life.

"Yes, she texted saying that Tushar is not well." The worry lines on her forehead deepened. "What could have happened?"

"Must be a seasonal thing, Priya. You are getting unnecessarily worried."

"You know, he is the answer to all our prayers. Whenever I pray for…, I pray for Tushar too."

"I know, sweetheart, I know." He got up and took her in his arms. "Don't worry, nothing will happen. I have identified a backup for Tushar too."

"Oh, Udit! What will I do without you!" She stepped forward and hugged him.

⸻ ⟡ ⸻

Well, well, well. Look, who is awake? Did you have a good beauty sleep, my dear, Major Armaan Joshi."

Armaan stared at the man. The man with whom he had shared most of his time in Amritsar for two years. Armaan wondered how Danish had tracked him? What had given him away during the extraction? Most of his gang members were either killed or captured. How did he hook up with someone like Trisha? Armaan knew everyone in Danish's coterie and there was no trace or association of a woman like Trisha. Although she had put his life in danger, he couldn't put that fact out of his mind.

"How does she fit in?"

"She?" Danish's smile vanished as he looked at the fat man sitting behind still picking his nose.

"Is she in your gang?"

"Got you, did she?" He chuckled when he caught on whom Armaan was referring to. "Earlier, I thought just to take out a hit on you. But you know, killing you in one shot was too easy, painless, and wouldn't have given me the satisfaction. So, I got her to lure you here."

"Where is she?" Armaan asked as a pulse on his jaw ticked.

"Are you kidding me…? Oh fuck! Can that happen?" He began to laugh, along with the guard. "Are you jealous of me, Sameer, because of that woman? Oh fuck! This is hilarious!"

Armaan stared at Danish. There was no point pretending now.

"Oh, you don't know! I could never…" He chortled with ugly mirth. "High and mighty Sameer in love with a woman."

"What's wrong with you, Danish? Control yourself, you might get a heart attack. She betrayed me and I want to watch her squirm."

"Oh, really? You can't touch her now. Her role in this is over."

A strange cold wave of betrayal began to swirl in Armaan's gut. Was she really with these goons? How could the accident be arranged? His guts were not ready to accept the picture being portrayed. No one could be that good an actress.

"I wasn't too sure about her when I had picked her for the job, but she sure delivered, my God. And my men told me that you really enjoyed the journey with her. You thought you were smart? See how she made a fool out of you. The great betrayer has been betrayed!" He beat his thighs and laughed again. "How does it feel, hotshot!"

"Why not just kidnap me? Why this drama?"

"And risk my men getting arrested or killed? I know you are IB, Armaan. I am smart enough to gauge a situation and act accordingly. I'll never underestimate my adversaries."

Armaan decided to change track and fell silent.

"You thought I was a mark for you? And now? Tell me who is smarter? How I have fooled you this time, Sameer." Danish chortled.

"I didn't know you harbored such a deep resentment for me." Armaan looked around assessing the threats and planning his escape.

"I didn't, but your treachery left me nowhere in my brother's eyes. Look at me trying to prove my allegiance, running for my life. Why did you betray us, bastard? Why?"

"You do what you have to do." Armaan shrugged.

"I trusted you, you motherfucker!" He was literally crying now. "You've made a fool out of me. I have fallen in my brother's eyes."

Danish was a sentimentalist and had blindly trusted Armaan in those days. "Don't you realize you were ruining lives of kids? Drugs and what not."

"I have solicited none of the kids."

"Your men do, you don't. But that makes it okay? You go on holidays with that money, Danish."

"Don't bullshit me, you bastard. You've been lucky but not anymore. I have you under my thumb, and soon you'll be groveling at my feet for your life."

"You got me. What now?" Armaan said in a casual tone, simultaneously looking for a way out of the room and the situation. He had his hands free and the small, sharp blade in his hand. He was not overly concerned about Danish, who was half his size. Add to that, his regular consumption of drugs had weakened Danish's body to a hollow shell of a human being. He was more worried about the man behind Danish, who had a gun and a knife. The man had been a wrestler and fought dirty.

"You have caused me a lot of grief, Sameer. Now, you have to make amends." Danish wiped his snot on his sleeve and continued, "But before that, I am going to set an example for the world to not mess with me ever again. If we were not hiding, I would have tortured you on the *chaubara*." He referred to the central meeting ground in the slum where most of the community festivals were celebrated.

"I'll come back in a while. Tie him to the ceiling," Danish said and left the room.

CHAPTER FOURTEEN

Mahi was shocked when she heard the hospital staff say that Trisha had texted them and had taken leave. Why hadn't she texted Mahi then?

The information from the hospital made Mahi call her cousin who was in the police department. She even called Nikhil from the office. Manish came immediately and sat in Mahi's living room, thinking how to tackle the problem.

"Something fishy is going on. I didn't have the courage to ring the bell again." Rocking the baby Riya in her arms, she told Manish, "If Tushar wasn't well, Trisha would have told me."

Manish nodded. He had met Trisha a couple of times and found her to be a level-headed person, totally dedicated to her brother and quite social. It was not routine for the siblings to lock themselves in the house.

"What if she is injured inside and can't call for help?" Mahi paced the living room.

"Don't get ahead of things," Nikhil said chewing on his nails.

"We have to open the house and see."

"We can't just barge into someone's house without any reason or warrant," Manish said.

"I have the house keys. She has given them to me and I know there is a problem. What if someone has robbed them and they are injured? Oh, my God! What if they have been mugged or are lying in a pool of blood?" Sensing her distress, the baby began to cry.

"Mahi, hold your imagination, you are upsetting Riya!"

Manish took a deep breath, moved to the balcony, and called up his boss.

"What if there is someone inside holding a gun to their head?"

"Mahi, Manish is going to do something. Nothing can be achieved by getting unnecessarily worked up," Nikhil said.

"Yes, you are right. Maybe I should cook something for Tushar. He'd be hungry when he gets here in the evening." She rocked the baby in her arms and went to the bedroom to settle her down.

DAY 15. AFTERNOON
FARMHOUSE

Armaan braced himself as Shiva got up and stepped toward him. Armaan had the handcuff open, but he kept his hands behind him as if still bound. With his ankles still bound, the key was to strike at the right distance, at the right time and take the man by surprise. He kept up the appearance of looking a bit scared, braced and wary at the prospect of being tortured.

Shiva rubbed his hands and bared his teeth.

When he was at half an arm's distance. He leaned down to drag Armaan up. Armaan swung out his left hand clutching the metal handcuffs, hitting directly at Shiva's eyes, then plunged the blade into his neck. Shiva reared back in pain and Armaan took the blade out and stuck it into his chest, simultaneously pulling out the knife from the man's boot.

The man staggered back and the blade came out, blood seeping into his shirt and jacket. Armaan took another swipe, but this time the bastard was ready and held his hand and gave him a jaw-crushing knuckle rap sending Armaan skidding back and crashing into the wall.

Armaan hid Shiva's knife beneath his body under the pretext of his arm being broken and bent at an angle, eyes closed in sham agony. Taking Shiva by surprise again would be a difficult task given that Armaan's legs were still bound. He would have only one chance to strike back. Luck was on his side when, with ego into play, so far the man hadn't called for help.

Blinded by pain and anger, Shiva pulled Armaan up by his collar and this time, Armaan plunged the big knife into his stomach, putting all his weight on him, pushing him down to the floor. Hitting with his fist under Shiva's jaw so that his scream was lodged in his throat, Armaan struck him again with the knife on the chest. The man coughed blood against his palm once, then went limp.

Panting, Armaan took out the knife and cut the ropes that bound his legs. With all the injuries and the lingering pain, it was a task to free himself. He panted and straightened his bloody fingers. Taking the phone from the man lying unconscious on the floor, he sent the SOS code to Karan, then smashed the phone with a hammer lying near the door. Karan would start from Delhi immediately.

Cleaning it on Shiva's shirt, Armaan secured the knife in his own sock. Then he searched Shiva's pockets. He found a driving license and a few tobacco packets. Pocketing the license, he flexed his muscles to get the circulation going. Apart from the gash on his leg, which might need stitches, he was in good enough shape to escape from whatever godforsaken place Trisha had got him into.

Opening the door, which hinged on a single bolt, just a fraction, Armaan cautiously looked out. He was in a basement. There was no one around. Soundlessly, he moved up the stairs to the door. The waning sunlight outside hit his eyes making him narrow his eyes into slits.

To his surprise, he was in the same premises, but not in the main building. This looked like an outhouse. The small wooden cabin at the back of the house with a narrow porch all around could have been constructed for a guard or a caretaker. The two steps made of bricks and mud were broken. There were track marks of a motorcycle on the clearing outside the cabin, which went across the house and gradually disappeared as the thicket grew dense after a few feet.

He knew he was just at the outskirts of the Sukhna Wildlife Sanctuary. He looked at the sun, gauging the time of the day and the location of the farmhouse. If he trekked the periphery to the southeast, he'd reach NH5.

No one seemed to be around. Did Trisha go back with someone? He could still not accept her deception.

No one could act depressed the way she had done at the hotel in Ambala. What if she was really a victim? What was her real story?

He crushed his curiosity for the lack of an answer and moved toward the house taking the cover of a few palm and *neem* trees. He had gauged correctly and it was the right direction. If everything went well, he would reach the highway in a couple of hours from where he could hitchhike to the nearest telephone and call Karan to pick him up.

Crouching on the side of the house, Armaan ran along the wall and tried to calculate the distance from the house to the fence and the time for which he would be left exposed to the elements. He estimated it to be two hundred meters from his position to the stone boundary wall. He spotted the palm tree midway that could hide him in case someone was on the lookout from the rooftop.

Armaan took a deep breath and was about to sprint when he heard the scream.

***

DAY 15. EVENING
GURUGRAM. NCR

DK's unlisted number rang while he was trying to contact someone over his laptop. Jadhav looked at the display and came to attention.

"Who is it?" Still staring at his laptop screen, DK extended his hand.

"Nayak," Jadhav said politely almost devotedly as he handed the phone to DK.

"Do you have any idea what your brother has done?!" The thundering voice annoyed DK. Nayak may have been the big boss for the others in the gang, but for DK, he was a close friend.

"I didn't sanction anything. We are not even in touch since the raids."

"He is holding Dr. Trisha Mehra's bother hostage and has asked her to abduct the IB agent you harbored for two years. Agent, whose name I gave you. DK, why did you tell Danish anything about him?"

DK held his head in his hand. Danish was becoming a burden around his neck.

"And by doing this he has exposed my man inside the IB too. Now they will know that we know about the infiltration at Amritsar." Nayak continued to thunder, "Do you have any idea what Trisha's brother means to me? How did Danish even come to know about Trisha and Tushar?"

"I have no idea—"

"That's the point, DK. You have no inkling what is happening under your nose. A security breach that you couldn't find, then couldn't plug, and now you brother is like a loose cannon, playing with my pawns on his chessboard!"

DK knew it was prudent to remain silent.

"Why did you let him meddle? Do you know he has complicated everything? Believe me, DK, if I go under no one will be able to save you."

DK stayed silent, thinking for a few seconds, then said, "We can always kill her and her brother and dispose the bodies."

"No!"

The force behind the negative answer blew DK's mind. If he was surprised at the vehement reaction, he dared not breathe a word.

"I want that child alive and well! No one's to harm that kid."

"Yes, of course. Whatever you say." What was so special about that child?

The breathing on the other side slowed down. "Tushar is being held at his home, as a hostage. We can still salvage the situation. Ask the man at Trisha's apartment to leave quietly and not come to Delhi for the next six months. And Trisha..." He took a deep breath. "Now that she has seen Danish, I want that woman dead. You have to trace her and kill her. You have to perform these two tasks successfully, DK. Later, I'll make arrangements to get you out of the country."

"Okay."

"Find your brother and... and you know what you have to do. Make it look like this has no bearing or is in no way connected to you or to me. This is important, DK. It's a matter of survival now."

"Yes, of course. I'll take care of it."

"Keep the boy hale and happy. I'm banking on you." The call was disconnected before he could reply.

DK glanced at Jadhav and wondered whether he was on someone else's payroll too. Jadhav met his gaze steadily and confidently. DK shook his head. In the past few days, he had begun to get afraid of his own shadow. This had to stop. He couldn't just hide indefinitely and be a sitting duck for the law-enforcement agencies as well as his own enemies. It was time for some action.

"Where has Danish enacted this fiasco?"

"Our Sukhna farmhouse."

"You knew about this?"

"Sumi called me this morning, you were asleep."

DK paced his office, sick and tired of sitting and feeling like a mouse in a burrow. "Get the car ready."

DAY 15, EVENING
FARMHOUSE

Trisha was sure she was going to die. Her limbs were not supporting the panic in her mind. Panic for survival. There was no energy left in her limbs. She sobbed from the pain in her heart and on her body, which the beast was inflicting on her.

She wanted to push that bastard when he was violating her in the worst possible way, but her hands were held in a tight grip. The man sitting on top of her was holding her hands in one hand while opening his fly with the other. Her top had been ripped in two when she had retaliated the first time and the man holding her hands grabbed her breast and squeezed making her howl in pain. Her death was inevitable. Wouldn't that be nice though? The pain would cease. She would be united with her family. She was sure her brother was dead.

The moment she thought of surrendering a shot rang out in the confines of the large room. The next second, the pain on her thigh eased as the man salivating over her slumped over to her left on the floor.

With a painful groan, she curled herself like a fetus and began to weep bitterly.

"Trisha, get up!" Armaan shouted, simultaneously searching the pockets of the man he had neutralized, and pocketed whatever weapons and cash he found. He also looked for any identity papers but found nothing.

His mind was frantically urging him to leave the house as soon as possible, but he was going to take her with him. It was a split-second decision to help her. He had to get to the bottom of this or his life would always be in danger. She could give him the much-needed information. Maybe she knew Nayak.

Spotting a phone lying in the corner, he quickly took the man's photographs from various angles. He spared another glance at her. She hadn't budged an inch.

"Come on, Trisha, move." But it was as if she hadn't heard him. She was trembling though, which meant she wasn't unconscious.

Once done, he hauled her on her feet, but her trousers slid down her legs. "What the fuck?!" The man had ripped her waistband.

He left her to take off his own belt to fasten her trousers. But the moment he left her she slid down on the floor again, unmindful of her semi-naked state. In that moment, he realized that she was past caring about her life. What had happened here?

He had taken a sneak peek in the other rooms on the ground floor but had found no one except Danish in the living room, unconscious to the world. It seemed Danish wanted a high before torturing Armaan, but was wasted. If Armaan had time, he could have pumped the drugs kept on the table into his veins and finished him off, but Trisha had screamed again.

"Come on, girl. Stand still." Hauling her up again, he fastened her trousers with his belt and pulled her outside. He pushed her inside the vehicle parked near the entrance. His car was nowhere to be seen and he couldn't go past the main gate, where he suspected more men were stationed. As he hot-wired the car inside the boundary, he heard the shouts from the main gate.

He hadn't spotted any other vehicle near the house, which meant they'd have to pursue him on foot. Thanking God Almighty, he pressed his foot on the accelerator driving around the house to the mud track behind.

After racing the car away from the house for a few minutes and making sure no one was following, he threw a quick glance at her. She sat slumped in the seat, clutching her stomach, tears streaming down her face, least bothered that her top was beyond repair and her bra and chest were exposed to anyone who would peep inside the vehicle. He wasn't too bothered though. Looking at the narrow dirt road, it was unlikely they would come across anyone.

"What happened there? I thought they were on your side."

She didn't respond, but let out a low mewl and closed her eyes.

"Trisha, get a grip! You are safe."

"My brother!" she moaned, then began to sob again.

"What happened there? Where is your brother? What about him?"

"They must have killed him by now." She made a sound as if someone was sawing her in half. "Everything is gone. Everything is finished."

"What did they tell you?" The way she was crying, it seemed her brother was no more. What was the story here?

He needed her to be up on her feet again. In this condition, she was a dead weight for him. "Did they tell you he is dead?" He took a blind guess while concentrating on driving and ways to contact Karan. "Did you see his body?"

At that moment, the vehicle sputtered, then coughed. He glanced at the fuel meter and groaned like her. His luck was swinging like a pendulum today. The car jerked forward for a few meters more as he pressed the accelerator pedal, then the engine died.

The sun had set. He glanced back at the dark forest. No one was pursuing them on a vehicle, but they could be, on foot. He quickly got down and pulled Trisha out. He knotted the two halves of her top in front. "Trisha, listen," he patted her cheeks, "Did they say your brother was dead? Have you seen the body? He might not be dead. They must be messing with you."

Something in her eyes told him that he was able to get to her. Her eyes cleared. She blinked and looked at him. He needed her to be on her feet if he had to keep both of them alive. As far as he knew, there were two more men left behind who could be getting reinforcement to track them down. "The murderous bunch that they are… they still won't kill anyone like that."

"He is so helpless and fragile," Trisha whispered so softly that he had to strain to hear.

"Till the time you don't see him, you don't lose hope. Okay? Maybe he is alive and he may need you. You have to keep up. Come on. We have to move." Armaan held her arm and pulled her into the forest. He had a fair idea about the direction and the area, and knew that a couple of kilometers to the West was a village where they could find shelter and Karan would be able to pick them from there.

"Why did you come back?" she asked softly, limping along with him, clutching her shirt at the nape.

He himself didn't know the answer to that question. All his life, he had gone by his gut feel and ninety-nine percent of the time, it had kept him on the right track. And his gut told him that she was also a victim, although the aftertaste of mistrust and her dishonesty continued to coat his mind.

All the speculation and churning of thoughts came to an end when a bullet whizzed past his head and ricocheted on the tree. The wood chipped and Armaan ducked pulling Trisha down.

CHAPTER FIFTEEN

Manish stationed his men at various vantage points around Trisha's building to get a glimpse inside her apartment, but even after two hours, they did not see or hear any movement inside. All the windows and doors were closed and the curtains pulled on them.

After talking to his seniors, he decided to enter the apartment. The layout was mirror opposite to his sister's, so his team had familiarized themselves with the space. He briefed his men about the operation.

Speed was the key.

With light, silent steps and wearing full riot gear, his team approached Trisha's door. Keeping himself out of the sight of the peephole, soundlessly, one of his men turned the key and slammed open the door. He rushed inside with his team. "Police! Hands up!"

They found an empty living room and a filthy kitchen. Manish frowned. As planned, the two teams slowly moved toward the two bedrooms. The doors opened without any resistance. And they found Tushar and Kishore Dada bound and gagged, lying in each of the rooms.

Tushar broke down sobbing and sniveling when he saw Mahi.

DAY 15. EVENING
FARMHOUSE

DK stormed into the living room of the farmhouse and found Danish drunk and stoned, half lying on the couch, the TV blaring some obscene dance number.

"What have you been doing, you bastard?" DK thundered and kicked his legs. "Where is the woman?"

Danish looked everywhere but at him and grunted.

"Danish, I don't have time for this. Where is she?"

"Who?" He blinked like an owl. "What?"

"Are you nuts! You are stoned! Why did you—" He broke off with a string of expletives. "You good for nothing pain in the ass." He punched him in the face and Danish slipped down on the floor.

Jadhav came in running. "Shiva and Kedaar are dead. Shiva in the basement of the outhouse, and Kedaar in the bedroom on this floor. Jadya and Kittu are not answering their phones."

"He has escaped! And where is the woman, you moron?" He kicked Danish's stomach once again and jumped back to save his expensive leather shoes when Danish heaved then puked all over the carpet.

"And this time, he took Trisha Mehra too. You have blundered and have created a massive problem for me, Danish. Again!"

He stopped shouting when he realized Danish was beyond comprehending anything, lying on the floor with saliva dripping from the corner of his mouth, then he whispered, "I got him."

"What?!"

"I got the bastard and now I am going to torture him for betraying me."

"Torture? He is gone, you bastard! Do you think you could have bested a person who lived with you for two years feeding information to the police about us right under your nose!"

"No, he is in the basement. Shiva is guarding him."

"He killed Shiva, while you were here scoring. Why did you do all this?"

"Wanted to kill him... but Jadya missed him…in the parking lot…and found him with this woman. Sameer was… was sweet on this woman… So I… so I… lured him here with her help, to torture him."

DK pursed his lips at his half-brother's idiotic plan and rued the days when he'd taught Danish the tricks of the trade. "Where is the woman?"

"In the bedroom."

"Did you talk to her?"

"Yes. Showed her, her place in the scheme of things."

"Did she see you?"

"What?"

"Were you wearing a mask while talking to her?"

"Mask? Why would I wear a mask? I hate masks."

DK took a deep breath to calm himself but it didn't work. "You know Danish, the only thing that can save us now is this." He turned around, pointed the gun at his brother, and pulled the trigger.

Danish hiccuped once then lay quietly even before blood seeped on the fine jacket he wore.

"Damn, damn!" DK doubled up in pain and sat down on the sofa with his back toward Danish.

Worried, Jadhav looked on. "Sir, we don't have time. If they have escaped the police can come here anytime."

DK stood up and found a laptop blinking on the credenza near the entrance. He pressed a key in random and the screensaver disappeared and Trisha's name came on in a login window, asking for a password. "What the fuck! God! From where did Danish get this?" He tried Trisha's name as the password but the laptop didn't accept. "Jadhav, search and collect all the electronics in the house, then prepare to torch the building."

⬥⬥⬥

DAY 15, EVENING

SUKHNA WILDLIFE SANCTUARY

"Trisha, on the count of three, we have to get up and run parallel to this log. Got it? Don't look back. I'll be right behind you." The forest terrain was tough, but they had to cross it before darkness set in.

"I can't," she moaned.

"Yes, you can. We don't have a choice or the time. One… two… three… Go… go… go!"

Taking a deep breath, she summoned all her energy and willpower, and ran toward the thick trees. He followed right behind her. The bullets rained on them one by one. Some ricocheted off the trees, some on the ground. Both the sniper and the gunner shot at them randomly. All of a sudden, from the corner of her eyes she saw Armaan stumble and fall.

"Armaan!" she screamed. One moment he was running beside her and the next, he was gone from her line of sight.

Unable to stop himself, he slipped down the mountain slope, skidding down until his fall was broken by the twin trees midway. Without a second thought, Trisha too followed him, slipped, skidded, and landed on top of him in the bushes. He grunted but pulled her behind the trees taking advantage of the slight depth wherein they had fallen.

"What happened… are you… hit?" she asked running her hand all over him.

"No." He shook off her hands and stepped back.

"There is blood. Are you injured?" She lifted her bloodied fingers. "Tell me, Armaan. Are you in pain?"

"Leave it be." He pulled his arm and stepped back as if he couldn't bear her hands on him. "Listen to me. This isn't going to work. I have to tackle them here only." She started to shake her head. "I have only one gun and no spare magazines. I can't take chances shooting at them at random. I have to hunt them down… I'll have to go."

"You are leaving me here?"

He pulled out the gun from his waist band and checked it.

"I understand you are angry with me."

He looked at her for a beat then said, "You'll be alright."

Her eyes filled up but she kept quiet. She knew she had lost the right to ask for his help.

He glanced at her, tightened his jaw. "I'm coming back. Nothing will happen. I'll just go around. I have to be behind them to get them off our back. One person pursuing us, we could have escaped, but we can't outrun two people with guns, especially because of your ankle." She frowned looking at her muddied sneakers.

"What if something happens to you?" she whispered biting her lips.

"You'd be glad, won't you?" He took out two knives from his pocket and put one in his waistband and the other in his left sock.

She dropped her gaze to her lap.

He held one of the phones out to her. "You will get a signal if you reach a meadow or a clearing." He continued when she took the phone without meeting his eyes. "It's just for… if we are split. But don't worry… I'll follow your trail and find you. We can connect using these phones when there is a signal." Saying that he tried to hide her perch behind the large stone with bushes and broken tree branches, and vanished.

Armaan went up the mountain quickly, taking a long zigzag route in the woods and reached a spot ten meters away from where he had fallen. He crouched down behind a tree and waited. He put all his concentration on just listening, filtering the sounds of the jungle. From his vantage point, he could also see the rock behind which he had left Trisha.

He saw something move to his left and heard the crunching of dry leaves as someone stepped on them. He slowly raised his gun and saw that the man was moving from his left to the place where they had fallen. The man inspected the skid marks and looked at the exact place where Trisha was, behind the rock elevation. The gun in the man's hand was pointed downwards. Armaan was right. They didn't have a clue about the forest or how to stay hidden while chasing. And that made everything easy.

Since he was not sure about the sniper's location, Armaan had to be careful to not have his location compromised. He shifted to his left, keeping the gunner in his view, and moved silently to the next tree and then the next, till he was directly behind the man. He put the gun in his waistband and took out the knife. Leaving his position behind the tree, he grabbed the man by the head and in one smooth motion cut his throat. The man went limp in his arms, choking on his own blood.

Using the dead body as cover, Armaan moved behind the tree again, dragging the body to the ground. He pocketed the man's gun and magazine, then searched his pockets and found a driving license and a wad of money, all in Indian currency. He was not carrying a wallet. He photographed the man, then scanned the dark, humid forest once again. Darkness was his friend as well as the enemy. He had spotted a snake camouflaged on a tree and worried about Trisha.

Trisha sat unaware and unsure of everything. Had Armaan abandoned her? She shouldn't be surprised if he had. She didn't deserve his help or… or anything. If he had left her though, she was sure she would die out here in the wilderness. Crickets chirped, mosquitoes buzzed, and she could hear wolves howling far into the jungle. She couldn't even run if she had to. Her whole body was throbbing and aching, her joints refused to move, and she could feel something crawling up her back.

The bushes suddenly parted revealing the muzzle of the sniper rifle. Her heart started to pound in her chest.

She stared at the round black metal. The cell phone slipped from her limp hand into the bushes. It seemed her heart had stopped beating, and she could hear millions of roaring angry bees inside her head. The only thought that came to her was that the man was so thin and young. He straightened his rifle and aimed at her forehead. She closed her eyes. Tushar's image floated in front of her eyes, then she heard the shot.

Trisha was jolted against the rock, but she didn't feel pain. She opened her eyes and saw the lifeless face of the assassin, frozen above her, blood oozing out of his forehead. The next second, his eyes rolled back and he keeled over her. A silent scream lodged in her throat. Trisha covered her head with her hands and closed her eyes.

Armaan came rushing down the slope, lifted the body, and turned it away from her. "You okay?"

Trembling, she pulled back her hands and looked up. He was sweeping the expanse of the forest intently. "What about the other guy?"

"He's neutralized," he answered dispassionately. "We have to move."

She stood up on one leg, taking the support of the rock.

Armaan rummaged through the dead man's pockets mechanically but didn't find anything. As with the other man, he also didn't carry any identification on him, except a driving license. He knew the license would be fake, but he pocketed it. He took a couple of pictures of the man.

"What kind of e-devices do you have with you?" he asked.

"None." She patted her pockets. "They had given me a locket, a phone, and a smartwatch. I left them in the living room when I was talking to that madman."

He pulled out the cell phones he had collected and frowned. Maybe they were tracking them using the GPS on the phones. He switched off all the phones, then picked up the sniper rifle. "Let's go. I have a faint idea about the area. We need to walk fast and reach a nearby village before darkness descends." He looked at the compass on his watch and began to walk.

DAY 15. NIGHT
MAYUR VIHAR. NEW DELHI

Tushar had been slapped and beaten, but otherwise he was fine. Kishore Dada had a fracture in his right hand and his ankle was sprained. They both were dehydrated and starved. While Tushar was taken to Mahi's place after first aid, Kishore Dada had to be admitted to a hospital.

"Oh, Tushar, Mahi Didi is here, don't worry." Mahi hugged him and took him into the living room.

"I want Trisha Didi." He stopped crying when he saw familiar faces, but he still looked agitated.

"Of course, of course. Would you like to have some *dosa* and *sambhar*? You like it, Tushar, don't you?"

"Yes." For the moment, he appeared to be distracted when Mahi brought his favorite dish and all the adults heaved a sigh of relief when he asked for Riya.

"She is sleeping. But you can play with her when she wakes up."

Later, when he went off to sleep in their guest room, Mahi called Manish again. "Where would they have taken Trisha? And why?"

"We are investigating. As per Kishore Mishra's statement all this happened on Friday night. There were two men, and Trisha was taken from the apartment early morning on Saturday. He didn't know anything else since he was unconscious on Friday night. But he told me that they were letting Tushar speak to her over the phone around meal times since Saturday."

"*Bhaiya*, please. We have to find her."

"Yes, of course, Mahi. It's our jurisdiction. We will leave no stone unturned. It's quite late, you take rest. You have to take care of Tushar too."

CHAPTER SIXTEEN

Armaan looked back and saw Trisha dragging her foot—her head hanging and her blouse torn. She had had it bad—the accident yesterday and then the attack by the bastard today. She hadn't complained throughout the hour's trek though. Was it just today morning that they were on the highway when he had called her a princess? Crap! He felt like a fool now.

What was her deal with them? Why had they turned against her? No matter what though, he couldn't be lenient with her. He shouldn't let their 36-hour long association become a weakness in handling her. She was connected to the gang somehow and till the time all the facts came to light, she would remain under the shadow of doubt.

A moan escaped her as he pressed on further.

Armaan stopped and broke a relatively straight and sturdy branch from a tree. He shaved off the small branches and edges, then held the makeshift cane toward her. She was startled and looked up at him, then at the cane he held.

Biting her lips, Trisha took it and blinked back the moisture in her eyes.

All of a sudden, it started to rain, soaking them. Everything seemed surreal. Trisha hoped everything was a bad dream and she would wake up in her bed, eventually laughing at her wild imagination. But it wasn't a nightmare, Armaan's arm soaked in blood was testimonial to the recent deadly attack on them, not to mention her own throbbing ankle and mud-soaked bandage.

It was getting very difficult for her to put one step after the other in her wet jeans and the thrashing she took in the hands of those criminals, not to mention the accident in Ambala. Her legs felt as if heavyweights had been tied to them. Armaan, on the other hand, kept marching forward with purposeful strides and boundless energy.

As they walked further, the trees began to give way to a clearing that led to the village. He stopped near a tree and began to dig with the nozzle of the rifle.

"What are you doing?"

"Have to hide the rifle if we hope to get a room in the village."

She just nodded, feeling drained and exhausted from the physical and emotional ordeal of the past two hours.

"Here," he took off his jacket and T-shirt, and held the T-shirt out to her, "They'll ogle at you and might think the worse," he added when she raised questioning eyes at him.

She looked down at herself. The wet, torn, blue blouse clung to her torso like a second skin leaving her waist bare. She took his T-shirt and pulled the soggy garment over her head. His smell enveloped her, making her feel warm and secure. By the time she straightened the T-shirt, he had turned and was fiddling with the compass on his watch.

Clad in a white under-shirt and jeans, with the gun stuffed to his waistband at the back, Armaan looked more like a forest commando. He pulled on his jacket covering the gun. She wondered if the villagers would be hospitable at all despite her being covered from neck to mid-thigh in his black T-shirt and he wearing the jacket over the vest.

Completely wet, they reached one of the small villages, at the edge of the Wildlife sanctuary, which came under the district of Chandigarh.

They finally spotted two teenagers fooling around with a pair of hounds.

"Can you take us to the head of the village?" Armaan asked.

Though the boys nodded and started on, expecting them to follow, they kept throwing curious glances at both of them.

The boys took them to a decent-looking cottage which seemed like a barn cum store. In the middle of the courtyard, a distinguished-looking man with grey hair sat on a cot sipping something from a large copper glass.

"*Namaste.* We were driving by, and our car broke down on the other side of the sanctuary. We sort of lost our way," Armaan said when they reached the man.

"Who are you?" The man asked.

"Major Armaan Joshi with Garhwal Rifles, Indian Army."

Trisha's eyes jerked to him. Major! He was with the Indian army!

"May I borrow your phone?" Armaan continued talking to the man. "Our phones have discharged. I'll call my brother. He will be here in a few hours to pick us up."

She'd never asked him his name or profession. Like a fool, she had believed everything those goons had told her. Or it could be that Armaan was lying.

But he was the one who had rescued her from them. Nothing in his behavior in the past three days told her that he was a man on the other side of the law. Oh God! What a mess.

The Sarpanch, the head of the village, was mighty impressed with Armaan and took him to his own home. He had a spare cottage inside his courtyard. He asked his wife to ready it for them and offered them tea. By the time they had tea, the cottage was ready.

His wife handed Trisha some dry clothes. "You should change out of these wet clothes and ask your man to change too. Are you okay? This looks nasty." She pointed to her ankle.

Her man? How intimate that sounded. Though Armaan hadn't introduced her, they had assumed that she was his wife. Of course, Armaan and Trisha had to pretend that they were man and wife. Trisha smiled. "I'll re-bandage it. It'll be fine, thanks."

"I'll send some medicine. He is hurt too."

Trisha's smile vanished, but she nodded. Thankfully, the lady had turned back.

"Let me take a look at your wound," Trisha said when the Sarpanch's kid brought some disinfectant, and fresh bandage.

"It's okay."

"It needs stitches," she said, as she eyed the injury where the bullet had grazed the skin on his upper arm. "It needs to be cleaned and bandaged at least."

"Leave it be," Armaan snapped as he checked the phone again, and stood with his back to her. "Change. You have five minutes. And don't think I'll leave the room to give you privacy."

Armaan had spoken with Karan on the phone he had borrowed from the Sarpanch and briefed him about the situation. It was eleven in the night. The local police was expected to reach the farmhouse in ten minutes and if his estimate was right Karan should reach them in two to three hours. It would be good to leave the place early in the morning before the rest of the villagers woke up.

When he heard no movement behind his back, he turned back and found Trisha leaning on the wall, staring out of the tiny grilled window of the cottage. The cotton salwar suit that they had given her was a size too big on her shoulders and really small for her height, but it was better than their wet clothes. She looked composed.

Someone knocked and handed him two plates with simple but more than enough food for four. He thanked them again and kept the plates on a small wooden table.

He then peeled off his clothes and wore the shirt and pants provided by the generous people and sat down to eat.

Trisha kept staring out of the window unable to fathom how to tackle the situation. "I'm sorry," she whispered after a beat.

He didn't say anything, didn't even look at her.

"Armaan, I had no choice." She finally looked at him.

"Oh, yeah!" he hissed. Even after all the help that he had given her, the sarcastic tone told her that he didn't trust her.

"I'm really sorry for putting you through this. They had my brother as a hostage, they might still have."

He ate, his eyes on the plate.

"Armaan, trust me, they have my brother and my very old acquaintance who helps me, who is like family to me. They are still in the house or maybe the goons have killed them…" She bit her lower lip, choking a sob. "Right now, I don't even know where and how they are. I had no choice."

"Every word you utter now makes me wonder if you are playing another game with me. I even doubt if you really are a doctor."

"It's the truth. I did all this to save them, my brother and Dada. Armaan, I'm really sorry. I did what I had to…"

He stared at her.

"As I told you, my brother is really helpless, he is just seventeen with special needs. They came to our house on Friday evening. They beat him and Kishore Dada, and threatened me. They told me I'll meet him when I brought you to the farmhouse."

"To my death."

She didn't have any argument for that statement. "I didn't have a choice," she whispered.

He pursed his lips and resumed eating.

"And he wasn't there. I don't know what to believe. I don't know where to look for him. Armaan—"

"Is Trisha your real name?"

"Yes. I have to find my brother. Armaan—" She stepped forward but halted when he raised his hand. "Armaan, please, I can't do this without your help. If those people knew you, then you must be knowing their hideouts too. I have to find my brother."

"So, now I am in cohorts with them? If you still doubt me then why should I trust you?"

"No, you shouldn't." Sighing, she went to lie down on one of the cots. What had she expected? He had been nothing but helpful and compassionate, and she had led him to his death. No matter how innocent she was, he would never forgive her.

Finishing the food on his plate, Armaan too lay down on the small cot. Karan would be here soon. Someone had blown away his cover after he had escaped. Someone from his department.

One by one, the faces of all those who were involved in extracting him out ran through his mind. There were three who stood out—two in the field and one in the control room. Who had sold themselves to Danish and DK? His eyes glinted in the dark. They'd have to weed out the traitor before any more damage.

A movement from Trisha's cot broke his chain of thoughts. She tossed and turned, not because of the cot, but due to a nightmare. She shook her head vigorously and tried to ward off someone in front of her. Then she began to scratch her arms and pushing as if pulling something off her skin. He didn't have to comfort her, he thought and turned over to the other side waiting for the dream to end.

"No," she whispered.

He took deep breaths and waited for her to wake up, but she didn't.

"No…no…" She mumbled breathing fast, and, all of a sudden, sat up panting hard.

The next second, Armaan was beside her. He caught hold of her shoulders. "Sh…sh… It's okay. It's alright."

"I can't move… I can't breathe…" She couldn't complete and gasped for breath. "I don't want him touching me."

He couldn't help but take her into his arms, "It's over. It's okay. You are dreaming."

"The hands… his eyes… I still feel his hands on me… feel their repulsive breath over my skin…" Her breath hitched.

"He is dead, Trisha. You are safe." He rubbed her cold arms, as she clutched his shirt and sobbed. "It's over." He stroked her back in comfort trying to warm her trembling body. She clung to him and wept soundlessly.

Slowly, her heartbeat became normal, and the tears stopped. Her violent sobs subsided to hiccups. She raised her drenched eyes to his, her lips trembling from the aftermath. A lone tear sneaked from her left eye and slipped onto her cheek.

Wiping the tear with his thumb, he leaned down and kissed her forehead, her eyes, her lips. Her arms crept around his neck and she clung to him as if he could ward off the unpleasantness she felt. She smelled of fresh rain and woman. His arms tightened. He wanted to bury himself in her. He knew she wanted comfort and it shouldn't go any further than this, but he couldn't stop himself. It felt so right together. She was soft, delicate and thin. He could span her waist with his two hands.

She sighed as the comfort seeped in and the nightmare faded. Her hands caressed his nape, then traced the line of his jaw. She leaned toward him and held his face and started to rain feather-light kisses on his face, tracing his jawline.

Hungry for her lips, he held her chin and kissed her full on. Her mouth opened inviting him for a more intimate assault. He too couldn't stop stroking and caressing her. The feather-light touch induced him to pull her closer to him.

And then, someone knocked.

Startled, Armaan swore and pushed her back. Cursing himself and his lack of control with her, he got up to open the door.

CHAPTER SEVENTEEN

It was shy of three a.m. when Karan knocked on the cottage door. Armaan had seen the incoming text from Karan on his borrowed phone. The gun ready in his hand, he opened the door and pulled Karan inside.

"Whoa!"

"Hope no one tracked you."

"I'll try not to feel insulted by that statement," Karan said before he spotted Trisha. His eyebrows went up as he looked back at Armaan.

Trisha had pulled the bedspread up to her neck when she had heard the knock. Her moist and swollen eyes darted toward Armaan, then came back to Karan.

"We have to get out of here fast. Did you bring the spare clothes?"

"Yup," Karan handed him a backpack. "By my reconnaissance, no one here in the village could cause trouble. My vehicle is on the dirt track to the left of this farm."

Armaan took out the fresh clothes and began to change.

"You both really took a hell of a beating. I'm sorry I didn't have any in your size." Karan handed her track pants and a sweatshirt.

"No problem." She took the clothes.

"We'll go out so you can change."

"No. Turn your back," Armaan said scowling as he turned.

"But—"

"It's okay." She turned to a corner, to take off the *kurta* the Sarpanch's wife had given her.

Karan dutifully turned his back as Armaan had.

"I'm ready," she told them after putting on the clothes. She folded the *kurta* set and placed them on the cot.

"Here's the cell phone you asked for." Karan handed Armaan a new cell phone. Armaan fastened the Bluetooth to his ear and connected it to the phone. It was good to have something through which he could connect with the HQ securely.

⸻ ❖ ⸻

DAY 16. EARLY MORNING
THE VILLAGE / NATIONAL HIGHWAY

Armaan woke up his hosts and handed them the phone, thanking them for their hospitality.

"Did you bring the handcuffs?" Armaan asked as they took the dirt track to the main road where Karan had parked his vehicle.

"What?"

"Handcuffs, Karan. Are you having a problem with your hearing?"

"Yes, I have them." He took out the handcuffs from the boot.

Armaan opened the rear door of the vehicle and gestured for Trisha to take the seat. When she sat down, he handcuffed her left hand to the handle of the coat hanger attached to the roof of the car.

Trisha looked the other way, blinking fast.

Karan wanted to question the act since he didn't have an inkling about the circumstances, but knew very well not to question Armaan in front of a suspect. He drove on the NH58 to Chandigarh, while Armaan sat on the passenger seat, ready and alert. After a few kilometers of watching the rearview mirror, Armaan relaxed.

"Have some." Karan handed him a bag. "I'm forever bringing you food."

Trisha shook her head when Karan handed her a takeout bag too.

"Eat," Armaan barked at her, then bit the apple he found in the paper bag.

Karan raised his eyebrows but mercifully stayed silent.

"We can't have you fainting when we interrogate you," Armaan said when she made no move to open the bag.

She pursed her lips and pulled the bag on her lap.

Karan spared her a glance. She looked a bit miffed by Armaan's rebuke, but otherwise, she appeared serene and composed.

"We have a tail," Karan said after half an hour as if talking about the weather.

Armaan narrowed his eyes and checked the side view mirror. A black SUV, with dark tinted windows, one vehicle behind them, followed at a steady pace. He took out his gun strapped to his ankle and released the safety catch. He then noted the registration number on his cell phone and sent a message to the HQ.

Beside him, Karan drew up his gun too. "We need to un-cuff her so that she can lie down on the seat."

Armaan exhaled. He knew she couldn't open the door since both the rear doors couldn't be opened from inside, but she still could cause trouble for them. It was going to take a lot from her to get his trust back.

Trisha's eyes went large as she saw the gun on his lap. She looked back. Her heartbeat accelerated along with the speed of the SUV.

"Keep your head down," he said, releasing her hands and cuffing them to the door handle, "And don't look back."

She tried to follow his instructions but her whole body was on alert.

Karan drove at a steady pace expertly maneuvering the vehicle on the narrow roads. His attention was on keeping the SUV as far away from them as possible. The oncoming traffic helped keep the pursuing vehicle in check.

The SUV trailed them at a constant speed for the next half an hour. It did not attempt to overtake but it also did not allow any other vehicle to come in between. Trisha was tired of slouching down and desperately wanted to stretch.

"They are making sure we are under their radar," Karan said.

"Maybe planning for an ambush later."

"Do they still have so many men around."

"Don't underestimate them at all."

Trisha looked at both of them, calm and composed as if criminals tailing them was routine, talking about a trap that could lead to their death—her death. Was Karan really Armaan's brother? Or just a colleague from the army? Given the circumstances, Armaan wouldn't have called just anyone.

From the way they spoke, it seemed Karan was in the force in some capacity. If that was the case, would he believe her? She looked outside the window and schooled herself to not worry. What could be worse than getting arrested and the jam she was in?

Karan drove the vehicle at normal speed as they entered the town. Trisha wondered when he took a turn into the local bus stand depot. Would they cover the rest of the journey by bus?

Then all hell broke loose.

He honked and accelerated as if trying to take off like a plane, scattering the hawkers, and passengers helter-skelter. Trisha gasped, held the back of the seat, closed her eyes, and prayed. He took a sweeping circle of the premises and shot out of the bus stand and drove back toward Chandigarh.

She hissed when her head banged against the door.

Karan was a man possessed now. He drove like a maniac out of the town and at the outskirts took a steep right turn, then drove deep into the dense woods and switched off the engine even while the car was in motion. The vehicle came to a stop deep inside the thicket.

Trisha straightened in slow motion. Peering from the side window, she saw that they were totally hidden from the road. She couldn't believe her ears when she heard Karan say, "Wow. That felt good."

They waited till an army truck arrived. Their identifications were checked, cleared, then they boarded the truck. The back of the truck had two rows of benches screwed to the container wall.

Armaan leaned back and closed his eyes, tired from running on adrenaline for more than twenty hours. Despite his best intentions to keep a distance, his attention went to Trisha again. She sat on the bench across them, staring at the handcuffs on her hands.

He knew putting her in handcuffs was overkill. But it helped him bring the focus to the events of the past few days. She had more bruises on her face and he knew she had new ones in other places too, including her mind. The sudden urge to beat the man who had put his hand on her into pulp took him by surprise. He reminded himself that he had already killed the man.

He glanced at Karan, who was watching him. Karan raised his eyebrows. Armaan leaned back and closed his eyes again.

How in hell's name was he going to walk away from her? How could she mean so much when she had betrayed him the way she had? She was nothing to him. Then why was he so concerned?

They reached the army cantonment in the morning hours without any mishaps. The police jeep was waiting for them at the army cantonment gate. They were whisked away inside a huge police station, a grim-looking building behind high stone walls.

⸻⸻⊰◈⊱⸻⸻

DAY 16, MORNING
LUTYENS, NEW DELHI

"Can I get something for you?" Udit asked when Priya came down to the family room from the upper floor. "You look tired, sweetheart. Don't take so much stress. Everything will be fine."

"Yeah, I know." She smiled and stretched her arms slowly. "Had a tough night?"

Udit looked at her and was overwhelmed with love. Her long hair flowed down her waist and she looked like a goddess in her ivory, silk nightgown with a matching lace kimono wrap.

"Pour me three fingers, scotch, please, Udit." She sat down on the couch reclining on the plush red and white cushions.

The house intercom chirped. "Yes." Udit picked up.

"Sir, I'm very sorry, but there is a man called Nayak, who wants to talk to you."

Priya gasped at the name, as Udit looked at her and switched on the house camera view on his tablet. The man was heavily disguised, but he knew who he was. "I'll be down. Take him to the library," he told the security guard.

"Is DK here?" Priya asked.

Udit sighed and nodded. Nayak was the code name both used when talking in front of others.

"Why is he here? We had agreed we'll never meet in person."

"He is losing it. First Danish and now… But don't fret over it. You relax, I'll be back soon."

Priya watched him go, hiding the deep lines of worry marring his handsome features.

"Why have you come here? What if they are watching you?" Udit hissed when he was sure that the library's door was closed and no one could hear them.

"I took all precautions and this brought me here." DK pulled out the laptop from under his coat and placed it on the table.

"Who's is this?"

"Dr. Trisha Mehra's." DK smirked. "Found it with Danish," he said in a choked voice, before he cleared his throat and continued, "I got it hacked for the password, and look what I found."

He clicked a few keys and opened an Excel file. "Look at the accounts of your sins."

Udit's eyes went wide as he recalled each and every patient who had passed through his hands and eyes in the top floor OT of the Delhi hospital in the past year.

"How was she able to extract so much information from the hospital, Udit?" DK asked. "You have been pounding at me for Joshi and now? Now you have a leak here, right under your nose!"

Udit Gaekwad paced his plush library and seethed. Bloody ungrateful wretch. Her father had come begging for help when he couldn't succeed in anything in life. And this was how she was repaying him.

"Is she an agent working with Joshi?" DK asked.

"I don't think so."

"You don't think so? I expected a better answer, Udit, since you have a man inside the IB."

"You are a fine one to talk, DK. That man is compromised because of your brother. And I'm not omniscient."

"And now she is with him, with the IB. And they will make her spill out everything."

"How will they connect Danish with this?"

"Danish to me to you."

"She doesn't know you, so there will be no connection. And this is just the receivers' records and the personal data is coded. There is no way anyone can break this code."

DK contemplated the scenario.

"And we don't have a paper trail, so this remains buried," Udit continued.

"It remains buried till the time she doesn't confide to them about this." DK waved his hand at the laptop. "What if she talks to them about her suspicions about these operations? If they get a whiff of this, Udit, they are going to dig. And dig they will, now that Danish has touched Rao's golden boy. And the golden boy has the hots for your doctor, your supposedly, would-be fiancé."

Udit looked sharply at DK.

"Yes. Danish had her wired and all their conversations recorded. They slept together the night of the CJI's daughter's reception where she was supposed to be your plus one."

Udit pursed his lips.

"My men tailed them on the Chandigarh-Delhi highway but lost them. They are deadly and dangerous when provoked."

"I'll take care of her," Udit said.

"We should bug her home and communication devices."

"I said I'll take care of her. Go now and don't contact me, for God's sake wait till I call you."

Udit then dialed a number after DK left and the library door was closed. His phone was answered on the first ring. "I want a trace on Dr. Trisha Mehra… Yes… okay," he said then disconnected.

"What happened, Udit? Is he gone? Is everything alright?" Priya entered the library.

"You don't worry your pretty head about anything. Everything is under control."

"Your men haven't been able to find Tushar is it?"

"The police took him with them last night. He is with the neighbor, all hale and hearty." His furrowed eyebrows indicated his stress and worry. "No connection to us."

"This is turning out to be too complicated. We'll have to bring in the backup, Udit."

"Yes, but he is not in India."

"Then arrange for him to be brought here." She turned to go then stopped. "And this time, he will live in the basement, as planned earlier. We can't take any chances."

"Yes."

CHAPTER EIGHTEEN

Armaan took off the moment the truck stopped inside the jail premises. It was Karan who took Trisha inside and stayed with her, while she was booked like a common criminal. Armaan's objectivity and indifference hurt. A lot. But then she understood why he had to do it. There were lots of grey areas in their relationship or association—or whatever it was. It was too complicated to define.

Her heart continued to skip beats as she was led from room to room. She knew her life was over when they told her that she was under arrest for conspiracy to kidnap and murder a federal agent.

They then recited her rights and obligations. She was booked at the jail, complete with taking her fingerprints and a photo holding a placard with a number like they showed in the OTT crime shows. She went through the motions like an automaton, giving them the information they asked.

"I'm entitled to one call."

Karan smiled. "Yes, you are." He pushed a landline phone toward her. "You get only one call, Dr. Mehra. Use it to talk to someone who can help, like a lawyer."

Trisha rang Kishore Dada's brother's number, but there was no response. Tears threatened once again as the phone went on to ring and no one picked up. Ideally, she should have called Mahi, but to her frustration she didn't remember Mahi's number.

She was taken to a holding cell, which was like a jail with concrete walls on the three sides and the front was solid, fat iron bars with a built-in door. Trying not to touch anything, she wrapped her arms around her torso as she looked around. The cell had a concrete bench with a folded blanket on it and a metal WC screwed on the wall. Spiders had made their colony in every corner of the roof. Everything was dusty and rusted at places, and revolted her.

Worried about everything and tired of her injuries she slid down on the floor, leaning against the concrete bench's leg, which looked relatively clean. A few minutes, later a man with a stethoscope and a box came inside.

"Karan says you are injured. Let's see." He placed the box on the bench and sat down on the plastic chair a guard fetched for him.

She held out her arm, that had the fresh bruise from the truck fiasco in Ambala.

"Quite a beating you took." The doctor gently examined, cleaned and bandaged all her visible injuries. He gave her a cold compress for her knee and re-bandaged her ankle, which looked more swollen than yesterday. Was it yesterday? Or the day before?

To her surprise, the guard then brought a sealed-tray that had a proper meal, complete with salad, pickle, spoon, and a paper napkin. She was sure criminals didn't get this kind of treatment. The sight of the sealed water bottle gave her some relief and hope.

"Anything else? I was told you were sexually assaulted."

"I'm fine," she whispered but to her embarrassment, her eyes filled up.

"Okay then, take these two painkillers after your meal, and you'll feel much, much better." The doctor smiled and relaxed in his chair. "If you need anything else, do let the guard know, I'll arrange for it. We don't have a female staff down here at the moment but don't feel embarrassed to ask for anything. At least we doctors shouldn't."

"Yes. Thank you." She painfully pushed the lump of tears down her throat.

"Eat up so you'll heal faster. I'll see you soon." He patted her shoulder and left.

Trisha peeled off the cling wrap from the disposable plate. Perhaps, the doctor was right, if she had to help her brother and herself, she had to stay healthy. Tears clogged her eyes again at the thought of Tushar, who would be feeling lost and confused without her, wherever he was. Armaan was right too. She had to believe that he was alive and work accordingly. She had to get back to him or bring him to her.

She would somehow get through this. Somehow, she had to make it right.

❖

She is alright. Her physical wounds will heal soon. Mentally, she's tough." Dr. Raphael came inside the observation room that showed Trisha's holding cell and noted his observation in Trisha's file. "Tough and mature."

"What did the team find at the farmhouse?" Armaan asked.

"It has been torched. As per the latest report from the local police, three dead bodies, including your buddy Danish's," Karan replied, reading from a file then looked at Armaan.

"I killed two, but I didn't kill Danish. He was high on some cocktail drug when I had left the farmhouse. I wanted him to be caught alive," Armaan said.

"Then I think it must be DK's work. He must be tying up the loose ends," Rao said.

"If he did, I'm not surprised. Danish was always creating trouble, and was his half-brother. DK hated his stepmother. There was no love lost."

"We have a mole," Armaan said, looking away from the monitor that showed Trisha slowly stuffing food in her mouth. She ate with single-minded focus as if getting ready for war. "Danish knew everything about me."

Rao nodded. "DK and the gang got the information after you were taken off the assignment and rejoined the office." They both knew that if DK knew about Armaan before his extraction from Amritsar Armaan wouldn't have been alive. "From now on this mission is Code 5, the information remains amongst the four of us, Junaid and Sharlee. I'm bringing her in for e-surveillance."

Karan placed a file in front of Rao. "These are the people from our department who knew about the operation when Armaan went undercover." He placed another paper on top of it. "And these are the people who knew all the details of his extraction. Three new operatives."

"I want them on surveillance, both e-surveillance, and on-sight. Get our most trusted team on this, Karan, I'll approve it."

"I have the mobiles from the farmhouse." Armaan dug into his pockets and placed four mobile phones on the table. "This one belonged to Danish. And these are their driving licenses and credit cards. The phone with Trisha Mehra, she says she handed it to Danish. She was also wearing a locket and a smart watch. Those were also handed over to Danish before a man took her to another room."

Karan's phone pinged. "Got the initial report on Trisha Mehra," he read from his phone, "she is indeed a surgeon at Zenith Hospitals, employed with them for the past ten months. She, by the way, has three medical degrees, MBBS, MS, DM, under her name."

Karan glanced at his audience then continued, "Our prisoner is highly skilled, and well regarded in the medical fraternity. Many swear by her magic fingers in the operation theatre. She has a brother, seventeen-years-old, special needs child, Tushar. He lives with her and attends the Apex School for Special Needs People, run by an NGO. Day scholar. As per hearsay, she is quite close to the twins Dr. Udit and Dr. Priya Gaekwad. At the hospital, Trisha had called in sick yesterday morning stating her brother wasn't well."

"Monday morning? Monday morning she was with you, Armaan." Rao looked at Armaan, who was frowning and staring at the floor.

Armaan nodded.

Rao then addressed Karan. "Get in touch with her area's police inspector and have him call me. Also, get her phone call records."

Karan nodded and went out.

"Lots of connections. DK with Danish, Danish and her, then she and the Gaekwad twins. Interesting." Rao narrowed his eyes. The Gaekwad twins had a family legacy in the medical field, not to mention connections with the royal family of the Junagarh state. Their grandfather and father were very renowned and revered professionals in the industry and had political connections too. They were powerful people and casting aspersions on them without proof would rage a storm in the high echelons of society.

"When did you suspect something was wrong?" Rao asked Armaan, his eyes still on the monitor.

"She was quite distressed all along at the delay. Then I saw a black van parked in the hotel parking. Someone was smoking inside." Armaan raked his fingers through his hair. "I searched her things that night, but there was nothing incriminating, except her phone. It was not a smartphone. She became a little quiet... er... uncomfortable, every time I mentioned that I will drop her at her aunt's place. Nothing major, now that I am thinking aloud, but my gut did say something was off. I attributed it to regular problems at work or the fact that she was traveling with a stranger and that her aunt might disapprove."

"Why did you go there with her, Armaan? Unnecessarily, putting your life in danger." Disapproval was etched on Rao's face, as he took a deep breath. For him, all the men under him were like his children, especially the Joshi brothers.

"There was nothing concrete. I had alerted Karan that evening and was always on guard."

"Also a bit sweet on her since the night of the party," Karan muttered, who had entered the room just then and had heard the last part of the conversation. He got a steely glare from Armaan.

"Shall we get her into the interrogation room?" Dr. Raphel asked.

Armaan looked at Trisha, she had finished eating and was staring at her empty plate intently.

"Yeah, Karan, bring her into interview room 1," Rao said and headed out of the monitoring room. "And get Sharlee on board. Text these numbers to her and ask her to get me the location details. One of these numbers is a landline number, so we might be in luck." Rao looked at Karan, who nodded and went out of the room.

"Be careful, though. She is highly intelligent and has studied psychology too."

He nodded at Doc's warning.

⸻ ❖ ⸻

CHAPTER NINETEEN

Trisha braced herself as the door of her cell opened and Karan stepped inside. The guard handcuffed her again. Her heart began to tremble at the unknown.

"If you will follow me, Dr. Mehra. Use this." Karan held out a cane for her.

"Where are you taking me?"

"Just for a chit-chat." The guard with the gun followed them.

Karan took her through a maze of corridors and opened the first room off the stairs lobby. The room had a desk and three chairs, and a wall-to-wall black glass window on one side. Trisha wasn't surprised to see her battered reflection in the mirror. She felt worse.

"Take a seat." Karan pulled out the single chair facing the door for her so that the black glass window was on her left. A bald, short man with sharp eyes entered, as she took her seat. Karan began to set up a camera on her right.

"Dr. Mehra, I'm Rao. We'll be recording this interview." He recited Miranda and her rights once Karan gave him a green signal, and asked her to introduce herself.

Which she did with her heartbeat racing and her palms going damp with every word.

"Dr. Mehra, do you need legal representation?"

"No, I haven't done anything wrong."

"Dr. Mehra, in what capacity were you present at the CJI's daughter's wedding?"

"As a plus one with Dr. Gaekwad."

"How do you know him?"

"He is my boss at the Zenith hospital."

"What is his role at the Zenith hospitals?"

"He is Chief Operating Officer for the hospital chain and also heads the Urology department. He takes care of the administration and also specializes in kidney transplants, especially the complicated ones."

"You came with him, but you left alone."

"Yes. I came in my car and we met in the lobby of the venue, then entered the party together. But I left alone." Her eyes dropped to her hands. Probably they knew everything about her.

"Are you involved romantically with Dr. Gaekwad?"

"No."

"You went to the party with him."

"Yes, but I am not involved with him personally."

"Do you confess to be a party to the conspiracy to ensnare Major Armaan Joshi and lead him to that farmhouse?"

She blinked at the man, who returned her gaze without any expression. "No," she answered.

"Weren't you there on the highway waiting for Major Joshi to help you, where your car allegedly broke down?"

"Yes. But my car didn't break down. They had sabotaged it, the people who had my brother and my close acquaintance Kishore Mishra, as hostages. I had to do what I did under duress."

"So you were a party to it."

She stared at him for a few seconds. "You know, I didn't want to say this but I'm here because of Major Joshi." She couldn't help but look at the black window before she turned back to the bald man.

There was a stunned silence in the room. If the man was surprised, he didn't show. "Is it? Interesting. How so?"

"Because he asked for a dance and I… I accepted. Then we met in the mall's parking lot on Wednesday and he invited me out for coffee, an offer that I declined."

Rao frowned. "You'll have to be more specific."

"The following Friday, after we met in the mall's parking when I reached my apartment, I found my brother and Kishore Dada bound and gagged, two masked men holding a gun to my brother's head. They said that they'll kill my brother if I didn't bring Armaan… er… Major Joshi to the farmhouse on the outskirts of Chandigarh, near the sanctuary. They said my brother will be brought to the farmhouse and will be handed over to me if I reach there with Major Joshi."

"How does this prove that you became a target because of Major Joshi?"

"I was targeted because they assumed he fancied me." Her ears began to get warm. "They assumed it'll be a cakewalk for me to convince him to drive me there if he found me in the middle of the highway with my car having a problem. They zeroed in on me because he singled me out at the party, then asked me out in the parking lot."

Rao sat looking at her file in his hands.

"Can I get some coffee?" She ran her tongue over her parched lips.

"Yes, of course." Karan, ever the good cop, smiled and got up to bring one.

"Why was Major Joshi specifically targeted?"

"I have no idea."

"You must have had so many chances to tell Joshi that you are under duress. Why didn't you?"

"I never knew he was in the law enforcement. They told me he was in their gang."

"And you believed them, but didn't believe him?"

"He took out a gun in the mall's parking lot and said someone was shooting at us… he had a gun… I didn't know whom to believe, what to believe after I saw that man holding a gun to my brother's head! Moreover, they had me wired. They were tracking me through those devices they gave me and they could hear and see everything. Initially, I didn't believe them, but they would promptly call me every time there was some disruption in the plan during the journey. It was clear that they could hear and see everything. I couldn't take the risk." She looked at Karan gratefully when he handed her a coffee mug.

She took a sip. "I think the locket had a camera. I had to keep myself covered even when I was in the washroom. I couldn't take the risk of not following their instructions. On one hand, there was my brother, a special needs child, on the other a stranger, who I was told was part of their gang."

Her gaze flew to the glass window, then came back to Rao. She placed the cup on the table and leaned toward him. "I was told he was part of the gang and had betrayed them. I didn't know anything else about him except his name."

"Yet, at the night of the party, you went to a hotel room with him, knowing only his name."

Despite tears gathering in her eyes, she went pink. She knew she wouldn't be able to escape or avoid that episode. Heck, she was almost thirty years old, and single. She had nothing to be ashamed of. Taking a deep breath, she controlled herself, took another sip from the mug, and said, "That night was an error in my judgment and I'm paying the price for it."

Rao continued to look at her.

She glanced at Rao her eyes filling again. "My brother might be dead by now. I'm telling you the truth. You have to believe me." She looked at the glass window again. "You've got to believe me."

"How do we know that you are not part of their gang and whatever you are saying isn't to save yourself, Dr. Mehra?"

"Those men tried to rape me!"

"How do we know if that was not staged?"

Trisha stared at him and a pulse began to tick on her jaw. "I have nothing else to say." She pulled back her hands on her lap and sat down with her eyes trained away from them, chewing her lower lip.

Rao looked at her for a few seconds, then left the room.

Raking his hair with his fingers, Armaan turned away from the observation glass and left the room.

It was all his fault. He knew by that evening in Ambala that something was amiss with her. He was on guard since then. Still, he hadn't taken the right steps. He was also concerned about her brother if he was not dead already. The way she'd spoken to him over the phone, it was apparent that she needed to hear his voice. He was a special needs child and would probably be distressed with unknown people around.

"She is telling the truth," Armaan said, coming back into the room, breaking his silence on Trisha for the first time since they had arrived at the headquarters.

"You are ruled out from giving your opinion, Armaan. You are not in a position to think objectively," Rao said.

"I was objective with her all throughout. I have seen her breakdown when she realized that we had to wait for two more days at Ambala. I can't ignore my instincts and gut feel. She is a victim. I think we must start thinking on those lines."

"Doc?" Rao asked Dr. Raphel.

"We don't have all the facts. She could be a lower-level operative with DK, who knows something but not everything. Or, she might really be a victim, as she claims, and Armaan here believes."

Trisha's head was throbbing by the time Karan had finished asking her the same questions that Rao had asked her for a second and a third time. Repeating the same events and scenarios again and again. Right now they were double-teaming her. She was also sure that Armaan and the doctor must be watching from the one-way glass window.

She had no idea how many hours had passed, but she knew what they were doing. She had studied Psychology. They were trying to find holes in her statement. But she didn't blame them. In order to help her brother, she needed them. She had to get through this ordeal for the greater good.

"Please, I need to go home, or at least let me call my brother. Please, I beg you. It's a request." She looked at Karan, waiting patiently.

"You are charged with kidnapping a federal agent, Dr. Mehra. You can't demand or request or plead anything except for your lawyer. You have to give us something."

"They called me so I could speak to him. I remember all the numbers they called from."

Rao slid a blank paper and pen in front of her. She wrote down all the numbers. "I can also help you sketch the face of one of the men, the one who seemed like the one in charge. And the one who is now dead. He died, when…" She glanced at the window again, then looked back at Rao. "He was there at the farmhouse. Apart from this, I don't know anyone or of any conspiracy."

Trisha looked up when the interview room's door opened again. A guard entered with a tray and a file. He placed the tray with cold sandwiches and a cup of tea in front of her and left. Was it lunchtime already?

Karan then placed a bunch of photographs on the table. "Do you know any of these people?"

She sifted through the bunch and picked Danish's. "This is the man at the farmhouse. He was calling all the shots there." Then she picked up one and concentrated hard. "I don't know him but I have seen him in another photograph… a younger version of the same man." She put a finger on DK's face.

"Where?" It took some effort on Karan's part to keep his face blank.

"Can't remember." She closed her eyes, concentrating hard. "Leave the photo here and just give me some time I will remember."

"Sure." Karan picked up the rest of the bunch and left the room.

"Did you hear that?" Karan's eyes were shining when they came back into the observation room.

Rao's phone rang. "Yes."

"Sir, Manish Thakur this side. ASP, Mayur Vihar."

"Yes, Thakur. I need you to check an apartment for me in Phase III. I'll text you the address. I want complete confidentiality on this. No one, absolutely no one should be privy to this information, apart from you and me."

"Yes, Sir."

"It's in your jurisdiction. If no one answers the door, approach with caution."

"Sir, is it something to do with Dr. Trisha Mehra?"

Very rarely did a situation render Rao speechless and this was one. "How did you know?"

"Sir, she is my sister's neighbor and a good friend. When she didn't show up for her morning jog with my sister yesterday, my sister was concerned and called me." Manish narrated the whole episode, down to the last detail to Rao. "According to the Kishore Mishra, there were two men on Friday. One left with Trisha on Saturday and the other left by Monday afternoon."

"Good job, Thakur."

"Thank you, sir."

Silence reigned in the room when he disconnected the call and stared at the phone.

"What?" Armaan asked when Rao just stared at his phone.

"She is telling the truth."

CHAPTER TWENTY

Armaan looked at the glass wall again. Trisha was sipping water and surreptitiously wiping tears on her shoulders. Angry at himself for not being able to judge the situation correctly right from the start, had him fisting his hands. He had been trained to observe. How did he miss the signs? He should have been able to save her from all the disgusting ordeal she had to go through at the farmhouse and now during the interrogation.

"So when do we let her go?" Karan asked.

"Immediately. With the promise that she tells us what she remembers as soon as she does," Rao said.

"What if she doesn't remember DK at all?"

"She is extremely tired right now. Maybe if she has rested well enough and knows that her brother is safe, she might remember something," Dr. Raphel interjected.

Armaan turned toward them. "With DK around, how can we make sure that they will not harm her brother and her again?"

"They are under no threat if you don't have an association with her."

"But they assume there is an association. They chased us from that village!"

"They were after your life, Armaan, not hers. I don't read any threat perception for her or her brother when you are out of the picture." Rao's tone brooked no arguments from anyone. "I'm going to wrap this up. I'll have to hand over the case to the NCB or the CBI will look into it. This is not under our department."

"We can't just leave her high and dry!" Armaan scowled spreading his arms wide.

"Armaan, I think you should go back with Karan and lay low and on guard."

"I don't—"

"You are dismissed, agent. ACP Karan Joshi, you are to escort Major Joshi to your residence and make sure he stays alive."

"Sir." Karan saluted and looked pleadingly at Armaan.

Palms fisted, Armaan stared at the monitor for a second, came to attention, saluted Rao, then marched out with Karan following him.

⬥⬦⬥

Trisha picked up the photograph and tried to rake her brain for that elusive memory. Try as she might, though, she couldn't recall anything. Her head was pounding with heavy gloom and grief, emotions and thoughts that she didn't want to acknowledge. She couldn't give up hope for Tushar. If something happened to him, she'd die.

The door of the interview room opened again and Trisha lowered her head, blinking back her tears.

"Dr. Mehra, we have some good news for you," Rao said.

Her head jerked up and the flickering flame of hope gained strength.

"Your brother has been found. He is in good health and is with your neighbor, Mahi Anand. And Kishore Mishra is also fine, although he had to be admitted to a hospital for an injury he sustained during the assault on Friday."

Her eyes welled up again in relief. She nodded and swallowed back her tears, but couldn't find her voice. Rao understood her predicament, so answered what he guessed would be her question. "You are free to go, but it will be helpful if you can let us know more about this man, whenever you remember it." He handed her a card with only a number on it. "You can call here."

She nodded.

"I'll arrange for a vehicle to take you home."

"Thanks a lot…" overwhelmed, her voice came out as a whisper.

A few moments later, Karan entered the room. "Ready to go?"

"Yes."

"Come on then. You can take the cane with you."

He led her to a police vehicle parked outside the building. Inside the vehicle was her overnight bag that she had left in Armaan's car. "You guys got his car back?"

"Yes. Yours too. The towing service had taken it to the service center. Someone must be driving it to your apartment as we speak."

"Oh, thank you."

"Least we could do under the circumstances." Karan smiled.

The drive was completed in silence. She was elated and relieved that the whole ordeal was over. Karan was probably thinking about the threat for his colleague, Major Armaan Joshi.

He stopped the car outside her apartment building and came around to her side and opened the door. "That's it then."

"Yeah, thanks a lot." She eased a leg out, then stood up, not meeting his eye. "Will you tell him? Er… will you give my message to Major Joshi that I am really thankful to him for saving my life, twice?"

"Sure."

Trisha nodded.

"Trisha!" He called when she took a step toward the gate.

She turned.

He came up to her. "Probably I shouldn't be saying this, but it's better to be warned. We, I mean bro and I, think that you should be careful."

"He is really your brother?" Her eyes widened.

"Yeah. But that's not important. He feels, and I agree with him, that it's still not over."

"It's not?" Her eyes widened, then she sighed and turned to go, leaving Karan feeling a little guilty and worried.

❈❈❈

DAY 16. EVENING
MAYUR VIHAR. NEW DELHI

Trisha had a teary reunion with Tushar. Even after two hours of continuously assuring and reassuring him that everything was fine, he refused to leave her side. She had to take a bath with the bathroom door ajar and had to constantly speak to him while she was showering.

She felt a bit normal after donning her faded dinosaur-print pajamas, which Tushar had picked up for her on her birthday some years back. She spoke to Kishore Dada from Mahi's phone, her own was not to be found, while feeding Tushar his favorite ice cream. Mahi got them dinner and Trisha was thankful since she didn't have the energy to stand in the kitchen nor did she have her phone to order food online.

Mahi had been a rock throughout, though they both had indulged in a quick crying jag when they had met, with Nikhil helplessly looking on. Mahi informed Trisha that her cousin, ASP Manish, was going to come over the next day to take her statement.

Using Mahi's phone, she called up the hospital's landline, because she didn't remember anyone's mobile numbers, and spoke to the Dragon. She told her that both Tushar and she had had a mishap and she'd rejoin the hospital in two days.

When she finally settled down with Tushar, who insisted he'd sleep in her bed, Trisha let her thoughts go to Armaan. Would she ever meet him again? Probably not. They were done with the coincidences of a lifetime.

He hadn't come to meet her after leaving her at the jail's entrance, but she knew he'd been watching her all the while from the one-way glass. Now that everything was cleared, would he want to meet her again? She didn't know. Somehow, that thought brought another kind of gloom.

Maybe someday, she could meet him over coffee and they'd laugh at the events. Or maybe one day… pigs will fly.

That was some food for thought and she drifted off to a dreamless sleep for the first time after four nights.

⟞•⟩◈⟨•⟝

DAY 17, EVENING
MAYUR VIHAR, NEW DELHI

Trisha indulged Tushar the next day too. He was extremely traumatized and needed a few fun-filled days. Deciding to spend the entire day with him, she read him stories and made his favorite dinner. Later in the evening, she sat with him to indulge in some drawing. He loved drawing stick figures and she too dabbled with art, and tried teaching him spray painting.

"My friends…" He showed her his latest labor of love.

"Oh wow! Who is this?" She dutifully asked about all his friends and was happy to know a teacher was amongst them too. "Would you like to go to school tomorrow, sweety?"

"Don't call me, sweety. I'm not a baby."

She chuckled at the exact response she had expected. "Okay, but would you like to go to school and meet your friends?"

Tongue in his mouth he concentrated on coloring their shirts for a few seconds, then replied, "Yes."

Trisha heaved a sigh of relief. He was still not going to his room. It would be better to go out of the house and repaint new memories on the canvas of mind. Maybe she could redecorate his room with some wallpapers and posters, and get a new towel set for his bathroom, something to do with football and tennis, his favorite sports.

"I'll make sanwich."

"You are still hungry!"

"I'm a big boy."

"Okay." Trisha sat looking at the figures in his drawing book. The figures sat as if posing for a class photograph. Something clicked and she remembered the photo which had that man. The man whose photo Karan had shown her at the police station.

Her heart began to drum maddeningly. She had seen the man's picture on Udit's wall! A class photograph and then at some scenic place. Was that man known to Udit?

Rao's team hadn't told her about the man, but if they had asked her to inform them as soon as he remembered something, it meant it was something important. That man must have had some connection with the man at the farmhouse, Danish, and perhaps with Udit too. Were they pursuing the same crime as she was? No, no. The IB was associated with resolving a threat to the country from the borders. Did Udit had an association with people abroad? Was it much more sinister than she had thought it to be?

The noise coming from the kitchen snapped her out of the scary stupor.

"Didi, I broke my knife." Tushar stood holding the two pieces of the plastic knife that she had given exclusively for him to use. It was good to cut the bread, but wouldn't harm him.

After Tushar went off to sleep, she dialed the number Rao had given her. The phone was picked up on a single ring. "Yes."

"Hi, I'm Trisha."

"Yes, Trisha."

"I remember where I saw that man."

"Okay, stay put for further instructions." The line went dead, confusing Trisha. It was going to be a five-minute conversation. Why were further instructions required? Maybe they wanted to ask her some more questions.

❖

CHAPTER TWENTY-ONE

"She called an unlisted number just now." The message on Udit's mobile read, after Trisha's call.

Udit then called a number from his unlisted phone. "Sending you two names. Take care of them," he said when the connection went through. "Without any trace, no witnesses. And you will be rewarded like no other."

"It's closing on us?" Priya leaned on an elbow and looked at him from the bed.

Udit stared at the phone screen.

"Do you think we are paying the price for our disagreement with mother?"

"Don't be silly."

"They say things have a way of coming back—good things and bad things."

"There is nothing bad between us, sweetheart." He looked up at her, masking the worry he felt. "Everyone is entitled to protect whatever is dear to them."

"Come here." She patted the bed beside her. "And hold me, Udit. I'm feeling so cold."

He left the phone on the side table and took her in his arms.

Armaan flipped the pages of the novel he had planned to read for the past two weeks, without following the story thread. His mind constantly meandered to Trisha and the events subsequently. Despite whatever had happened, he couldn't shake off his concern for her. Especially when the four of them, including Rao, had concluded that she was indeed a victim.

What if anything happened to her? He had done his own survey of her apartment complex and knew there was only one entrance being used—others were closed—and Rao had posted a policeman in plain clothes outside the gate as a street-hawker. Manish was also instructed to make regular rounds of the area.

But posting just one policeman wasn't enough. What if someone got in scaling the boundary? Trisha herself had lots of injuries, that hadn't healed the last he laid eyes on her. Even if she recovered, what could she do in front of trained gun-toting gangsters? His heart seemed to choke at the scenario, so he got up and stood near the window, but there was no respite. Rao had ordered him to take rest. *Rest?* He scoffed. Sitting idle like an old man frustrated Armaan. He wanted to be in the thick of things.

After a few hours of deliberation and pacing Karan's old carpet, he reached a decision. He might get court-martialled for this but it would be worth it.

Changing into black jeans and a black T-shirt, he pulled on his combat boots, strapped a gun on his shoulder holster and another on his ankle. He took two of his knives and shoved them in his boots. He checked the battery of his cell phone, took a backup, and pushed them in his back pocket. He packed the electronic surveillance equipment that he had been issued and came out of his room.

"Going somewhere?" Karan entered the living room and found him picking up the bike keys.

"I can't sit idle."

"Normal people sleep at night."

"I can't."

"*Bhai*, please change and go off to sleep."

"It doesn't feel right. What if something goes wrong?" Armaan ignored his exasperated drawl.

"We follow orders."

"Okay." He sat down on the couch, jiggling his knee.

"*Bhai*, please. You'll get court-martialled and I will get suspended."

"Nobody gets suspended for driving a vehicle at night."

Karan sighed. "Yeah, that's a thought."

"Do you have a bulletproof vest?"

"You bet."

"Get ready then."

⸻◦⊰⟡⊱◦⸺

DAY 17, MID-NIGHT
MAYUR VIHAR, NEW DELHI

Trisha's eyes snapped open. She looked at the digital clock on the side table. It was three a.m., barely four hours since she had managed to drift off into an uncomfortable slumber. Something had woken her up. She glanced at Tushar, who was sound asleep on the twin bed. Maybe it was some dream or maybe the stress and adrenaline were not letting her sleep. Or maybe—

There, she heard it again, a faint rustle. Maybe it was just the breeze rustling the leaves, but after connecting that man with Udit and Karan's warning, she shouldn't ignore the sounds. Her joints protested when she got up. Not bothering with the cane, she hobbled across to the window that overlooked the small play area of their complex.

With a silent yelp, she jerked back when she saw someone crossing the green patch. It could be anyone, a guard or a maintenance person. After her ordeal at the farmhouse, she had been jumping over the simplest of simple things. Gathering courage again, she held the curtain and peered down. In the yellow light from the half-mast bulb, she saw him again. The man would not have alerted her, but the next second, he took cover behind the palm tree.

She shrank back against the curtains. That was unexpected from a normal man!

As silently and as fast as she could, she stepped toward the bedroom door and picked up her new phone from the side table. Mahi had made her enter Manish's number when she had come back. In fact, Trisha had memorized both Mahi's and Manish's numbers, but she had to be absolutely sure before calling them. It would be foolish to raise a false alarm.

She opened the door to her room fractionally and heard the faint click of the apartment main door. Heart in her mouth, she stepped back, latched the bedroom door, and slid a chair beneath the handle. She took the kitchen knife, which she had kept under the bed since she had come back, in her hand. She won't die just like that. She would fight them for her brother. Her eyes on the latch of the door, she limped backward when she heard steps approaching her room. A couple of seconds later, someone twisted the handle. Her heart leaped into her throat.

The door handle rattled again, a little more forcefully, but held fast against the chair. She stepped back again, colliding with something hard before a hand closed over her mouth. Her pounding heart dived into her stomach.

"Trisha…" he whispered in her ear, putting his other hand securely around her trembling body. "It's okay. It's me."

Startled, she gasped against his hand and leaned into him. Relief flooded through her veins. All her fears and tension melted away as she took strength from his hard length. How and when did he enter her room?

"I'll take off my hand, okay?" he whispered. "Don't make a sound."

Heart pounding, she nodded and the hand lifted away as she turned. "How come—"

Armaan placed a finger on her lips and glanced at Tushar who hadn't stirred. He stepped soundlessly to the door and put his ear to the door. Someone was fiddling with the lock.

Stepping up to her, he muttered in her ear, "Stand near the switchboard beside the door. The moment the door opens you switch on the lights—all the lights."

She shook her head waving her hand between the door and Tushar.

"I'll cover him," he mouthed and took a stance between the door and the bed, shielding Tushar.

She shook her head.

"Go! I'm wearing a bulletproof jacket." He pushed her toward the switchboard.

Acutely conscious about the danger and that anything could go wrong, they waited for the intruder to finish picking the lock. Trisha glanced at Armaan, who had the gun pointed at the door, and looked at nothing but the door handle.

The door handle turned fully and the intruder opened the door slowly. Trisha hit all the switches and Armaan said in a calm, steely voice, "Hands up or you are dead."

Trisha didn't recognize the man who stood there stupefied, blinking like an owl.

"If he doesn't kill you, I will." Karan appeared from behind the man with his gun trained at his head.

"Bend down. Slowly. And keep the weapon on the floor," Armaan ordered.

The intruder loosened his grip on the gun as he leaned down. The next second, however, he tightened his grip again and straightened. Trisha ran toward Tushar. Two shots rang out. She heard two thumps.

"What the fuck!"

She heard Karan.

"Oh my God!" Trisha pivoted and looked at the threshold to see the man lying on the floor—his head toward the living room and legs facing her, blood leaking from his head and leg, and Karan too was on the floor behind the man.

"Karan!" Armaan ran out jumping over the body. "Are you all right?" He pulled him up. "I shot him in the leg when he moved. Did I hit you?"

"No, you didn't. You hit the target. He shot himself. The bullet went through him and hit my vest." As Karan was getting up, a couple of policemen came running inside.

Trisha heaved a sigh of relief when she heard Karan mention the bullet-proof vest, blocking the view from Tushar, who stirred. She slid the knife in her hand below the bed before Tushar could open his eyes.

"Wha happen?" Tushar growled softly, half lying on the bed. "Too much light."

"Nothing. I had to go to the bathroom. You go back to sleep."

"No, who is that man?" Tushar pointed at Armaan. He hadn't yet spotted the dead man sprawled half into the room. Thankfully, only the man's legs were visible.

"He is my friend." She looked back. "Armaan, can you switch off the lights, please?"

"I don't want to sleep." Tushar insisted on getting up, as Armaan switched off the lights plunging the room into darkness. "Someone is in the livin wroom."

"They are my friends, Tushar." She reached forward and switched on the night lamp near the bed. From the corner of her eyes, she saw the body of the man being dragged out.

"No. Only Mahi didi is your frien." Sensing something wrong, he pouted and wrapped both his arms around her neck. "You said lying is sin."

"We met on a trip," Armaan interrupted. "Trisha, you both need to come with us to a safehouse."

Surprised, she looked at him blankly.

"You both need to get ready fast. No one should know. I'll explain later."

"I'll have to inform Mahi."

"We'll do it. Come on, pack the essentials you need, including your medicines."

"You said, lying is sin," Tushar held her arm and wouldn't let go.

"If it is for the benefit of someone, it's not," Armaan said. "Come on, we are going on a quest."

"Quest?" He let go of Trisha. She hurried to the cupboard and began stuffing things in a duffel bag.

"Yes."

"I don't want to go."

Armaan pursed his lips and looking clueless.

"I don't like quests. We get hurt."

"No one will hurt you as long as you are with me."

"How come?"

Now how do you answer that question? He looked at the boy who was his height but had the eyes and innocence of a child.

"How come?" he asked again.

"Because we are strong," Karan said, entering the room. "Hi, I'm Karan."

"Tusha," he introduced himself. "How come?"

"How come what?" Karan had lost track of the conversation.

Trisha smiled as she picked up Tushar's school backpack, which would keep him occupied wherever they were taking them.

"How come you are stron?"

"Come let's go. I'll tell you in the car," Karan said pulling his hand.

"Whose car?"

"My car."

"I'll have to change my clothes."

"No, you look quite handsome in that…" Karan led him out of the house, chattering nineteen to a dozen and Armaan and Trisha followed him out.

Tushar, sitting in the back seat with her, continued his conversation with Karan, who drove and also answered his questions with impressive patience. It gave Trisha the space to make some sense of the chaos that was her life right now. Someone had sent a man with a gun to her house. Was it because of that man she had remembered? Were the Gaekwads involved too?

She was grateful, though, because even though danger still loomed on her mind, she didn't feel as helpless and unsafe now.

Trisha was acutely conscious of Armaan too, sitting in the front, lost in his thoughts. She continued to think about what he thought about the whole situation. How did he enter her bedroom? Was he still angry with her? From the way he was helping her, it didn't seem like that. But he could be doing what he had been ordered to do. There was nothing personal in catching criminals. This was what they did at the Intelligence Bureau.

DAY 17, MID-NIGHT
RAO'S HOUSE, NEW DELHI

Rao's phone rang waking him from a deep slumber, but he didn't mind. He thrived on the challenge the job threw at him all the time. His dedication to the job was the reason for his divorce right at the start of his career. He never regretted it though.

"Yes, Armaan… Okay. Yes, right. A safe house is the best resort at this point."

He disconnected the call and thought for a while, then dialed an unlisted number. "Sir, I would like to take Dr. Trisha Mehra's case to a logical end… … yes, Sir… Yes, Sir… We'll be discreet and work with minimal resources… yes, Sir. Once we are sure of a connection, I'll disclose everything to the CBI, but for now it's only the six of us… No, no, no other mission will be compromised. Yes, Sir. Thank you, Sir."

He disconnected and called another number. "Sharlee, arrange for a conference call with the team on Trisha Mehra's case. It is still Code 5, only six of us will be privy to all the information."

CHAPTER TWENTY-TWO

They reached the safe-house, which was an independent villa in South Delhi. The door of the adjoining garage opened. Karan took the vehicle inside and the gate closed without a sound, shielding them from the danger for the time being.

From the garage, a door on the right led them to a storeroom, then to the open kitchen, which was separated from the living room by a marble counter. With so many bizarre things happening around her, Trisha had finally given up on solving this puzzle. It was all very confusing. For now, it was enough that at least she was together with Tushar, who, right now, was hiding behind her as a woman came out of a small room off the living area.

"Hi, I'm Sharlee." The petite girl, in black trousers and a white shirt, smiled at the siblings.

"Sharlee, the great," Karan remarked as he entered with some provisions which were in the car. "Good to see you again. Trisha, Sharlee here is a whiz with electronics, surveillance, hacking, and whatnot. Name anything in the field of IT and computers, and Sharlee is your go-to girl," Karan said, "And Sharlee, this is Dr. Trisha Mehra and her brother, Tushar, our guests."

In the time that Trisha introduced Tushar to Sharlee and Karan, Armaan went upstairs.

"The bedrooms are upstairs. Take the one to your right from the lobby," Sharlee said, "it has all the things for your daily needs. If you need anything else, make a list and we will get it for you. The kitchen is through here. We can take turns to cook or make our own. We are fine with anything."

"Gosh, you are tall, champ." Karan thumped Tushar and shook his hand, then winced. "My God, what a grip! And I thought we were picking a kid. No offense, Trisha."

"None taken." She smiled ruffling Tushar's hair. "We are all very tall in my family."

"Yes. Tall," Tushar repeated hugging Trisha again. "Big Man didn't say hello."

"He is a bit shy," Karan said, making Sharlee chuckle.

"Well, get settled then, boss wants a debrief," Sharlee informed them.

"Everything is in order upstairs. It's a little crowded down here," Armaan said coming down, looking at everyone but her.

Trisha guessed that was her cue to take Tushar and scram upstairs. She pulled Tushar toward the stairs, but he didn't budge.

"I don't like you." Tushar scowled at Armaan.

Trisha gasped as Karan chuckled and Sharlee stifled a giggle.

"Good to know." Armaan nodded and went into the small room that served as the control room. What else could he have said?

"Meeting in an hour," Sharlee informed them.

"Okay," Karan said and Armaan just nodded.

"Do you need to settle him down or something?" Sharlee asked Trisha. "Boss wants to meet you too."

"Sure, will be down soon." She pulled at Tushar's arm again and this time he obliged, though she knew that with all the excitement, expecting Tushar to sleep again was impossible.

They took stock of the small yet pleasant room with twin beds. Tushar flopped down on the bed but watched each and every corner with suspicion. Trisha had to open every *almirah* and drawers to allay his fears. After satisfying Tushar, she went into the bathroom to freshen up and to her horror realized that she was wearing her faded dinosaur pajamas. She looked like a street urchin with her black and brown bruises and night gear. What must they be thinking?

She quickly put on jeans and a T-shirt, and made Tushar change into day clothes too. As she had thought, he refused to sleep or leave her, so she had to bring him down. No one was around. She put on his favorite movie on a streaming platform and gave him a can of Coke from the kitchen as he demanded, fully aware that he was getting spoilt. It would be difficult to get him into a normal routine when all this was over.

She looked up as Armaan came into the living room from the small room. An awkward silence reigned in the room as they looked at each other, then she dropped her gaze to the TV control she had been holding. Armaan lingered, then paced back and forth between the kitchen and the living room. She glanced in his direction when he finally stopped near the refrigerator.

"I can't thank—"

"I'm sorr—"

They both spoke at the same time, and Tushar grabbed her arm again.

"Go on," he said, his eyes regarding her impassively.

Was it over? Was he no longer interested in her, now that he had seen the burden of her responsibility? Ignoring the depressing thoughts, she said, "I… " she began, but nothing came out. She cleared her throat and said, "I can't thank you enough for what you've done for me." She tried to get up since Armaan was standing, but Tushar wouldn't let her. "And I'm really sorry for putting your life in danger. And—" Overwhelmed, the words dried in her throat.

Armaan took a deep breath and ran his hand through his hair. "And I'm sorry for treating you like a criminal on the way back." His eyes went to Tushar, who had let out a snort the moment he uttered the word 'sorry'.

"No, no…" She looked at Tushar too. He was alternatively looking at the TV and scowling at them, no longer interested in the movie.

"How is the ankle?"

"Healing well." She stretched her leg and looked down, an excellent excuse to evade his eyes. "Not troubling me anymore. It's a little stiff, though."

"Didi—" Tushar interjected.

"By the way, how were you able to enter my room?" she asked, looking at him again.

"Through the bedroom balcony."

"You climbed four floors up! How?"

"We are trained." He sighed. "Look, Trisha. We have to talk. But this is not the right time or the place."

Hope rose again, and she bit her cheek.

"Are you smiling?" Armaan's eyes narrowed.

"No, no."

"I want to sleep." Tushar stood up.

"Yeah, okay," she uttered the words automatically and finally stood up.

Armaan let out a long breath. "See you then," he said and went into the small room, where Sharlee and Karan discussed something in a hushed tone.

"Did the Mayur Vihar police identify the man in Trisha's apartment?" Armaan asked Karan when Sharlee was setting up the call.

"A killer on hire, street name Cheema. Mile-long history sheet."

"Any connection to Gaekwad or his associates?"

"Manish's team is tracing the associations."

"Hmm…"

Karan's phone pinged and he was momentarily distracted, then his eyes widened.

"What happened?" Armaan asked.

"Sunil, one of our three suspects, was found dead under the HUDCO *Chowk* flyover. There. We have our mole," Karan muttered. "Bastard."

"They are tying the loose ends." Armaan let out a deep breath again and glanced at the stairs.

"You need some privacy? I can babysit," Karan asked tongue in cheek.

"Get lost."

"Guys, we are connected," Sharlee called out.

⁂

"Is everyone here?" Rao asked looking at the team in his office—Dr. Raphel, Junaid—and Armaan, Karan, and Sharlee on the video call.

"Yes, Sir. Dr. Mehra will be joining in a while."

"Okay, Sharlee, let's begin."

"First up, the text from Dr. Trisha Mehra's mobile. There were no calls taken or made from her device from Friday evening to Monday morning. It was switched off for the entire period, except for that one text. Her phone was switched on, on Monday. The text message was sent to one Ms. Susan Paul at Zenith Hospitals from the mobile tower in Chandigarh, and then the phone was switched off again."

"Okay." Rao had expected this since Armaan had told him that Trisha didn't have a smartphone during the journey to the farmhouse and back.

"The mobiles that Armaan retrieved from the Sukhna farmhouse had an app—an unknown, unverified app— installed on all of them," Sharlee continued, "I have hacked the app and have found these eleven user IDs, of which if we remove DK and the gang members who are dead, there are only five left." She displayed the IDs on the screen that they were using for the video call. "I've put a trace on all of them. If they communicate using this app, I'll be able to trace their locations."

"I don't think they will use this app anymore," Junaid said.

"Yes, even I think so," Dr. Raphel concurred.

"But keep at it, Sharlee and report to me the moment you zero down on a location or an identity," Rao said.

"Yes, Sir."

"Any progress on financial transactions with DK's companies?"

"Yes, Sir. I have been able to trace 75% of the transactions. The money bounces all over the world in different banks before it is parked in two overseas bank account. Some of it is coming back to India, I still have to trace it since it is bouncing to shell companies with bogus identities again before being transferred."

Rao nodded. "Good job. Do let me know the moment you come to a logical proof about the money trail."

"Sir."

"Junaid?" Rao turned to Junaid.

"Sir, Jadhav was sighted near the farmhouse that Monday. I feel DK definitely had a hand in killing Danish for going against him. If left to DK, he wouldn't have touched Armaan with a bargepole, let alone blackmail Dr. Mehra to hurt him. Danish was a fool with resources and he blundered. The NCB and the local police in Chandigarh are still looking for DK and Jadhav. So far there is no chatter of him leaving India."

"Now that Trisha Mehra remembers that photo, we'll have some fresh leads," Sharlee said.

When Trisha came to the room, she was impressed.

Sharlee had converted the whole room into a command center. Along one wall were the five monitors displaying the live feed of the perimeter of the house. The transmission was recorded round the clock. Another wall had three computers, where one of the screens showed a location map and one had a green cursor blinking on a blank screen and the third one, a laptop, was what Sharlee used to set up the video call with Rao and Dr. Raphel.

"Hello, Dr. Mehra. Hope you are doing well," Rao began.

"Yes, thank you. Please call me Trisha."

"You must be wondering and worried about what's happening around you."

She attempted a smile. "Yeah… seems like the apocalypse has descended on my otherwise normal existence."

Rao sighed. "True. We won't be able to help you right now with answers, because things are not clear even to us. But you were right, your ordeal at the farmhouse was because of your chance meetings with Armaan."

It was an effort not to glance at Armaan, who was sitting behind to her left, so she dropped her eyes to her hand, pinching her finger.

"We'll be able to tell you more once you tell us about that man in the photo," Rao continued in the same gentle tone.

Back to neutral ground, she raised her eyes to the screen. "I remembered seeing him in a group photo with Dr. Udit Gaekwad. From the photo it looked like they were on a college outing… a group of young men at a hill station."

Everybody's eyes on the screen became alert as if an electrical current had run through all of them.

"Sharlee, dig out DK's and Udit's college records."

"Sir," Sharlee immediately opened another window on the other computer.

Trisha wondered who DK was even as her heart began to race, her mind full of questions, but she held her peace. What had this got to do with Udit and her ordeal last weekend? Should she tell them about her own suspicions?

"So, DK and Gaekwad… could he be interacting with the gang as Nayak, so that there is minimal suspicion?" Karan commented rubbing his forehead.

Trisha's head jerked up, "What did you just say? The name…"

"Gaekwad? Nayak?"

"Have you heard the name?" Armaan asked, "Do you know anything about him?"

Trisha looked up and glanced at Armaan. "Dr. Ranjit Nayak Gaekwad, Priya and Udit's grandfather, the founder of the first Zenith Hospital in Delhi."

⟐

DAY 18. NOON
LUTYENS. NEW DELHI

"**Report**. Where's Mehra and the boy?"

"She was taken out, to a safehouse, I guess. Rumor is that the IB is involved again. Cheema killed himself on the spot. And, Sir…"

"Yes."

"DK has made plans."

"Take care of him."

"Okay," Jadhav said and disconnected the call.

Udit Gaekwad felt another wave of anxiety and nausea threatening to rise in his chest as he placed his phone back to charge. Everything was falling apart like a set of dominoes. He rubbed his chest and paced the living room.

This was all because of that one bad link in the chain, Danish. He brought in the IB agent, then involved Trisha. But then, Trisha was involved in any case, with her snooping and spying—always asking questions.

That was the reason he wanted to keep her close. Bloody bitch. She would have been nothing if they wouldn't have given the job to her mediocre father. Living in that slum all her life. She should have been grateful and loyal for all they had done for her.

Ungrateful bunch of street rats.

⸻⟡⸻

DAY 18. NOON
SAFE HOUSE. NEW DELHI

"**Nayak** could be an alias used by Udit Raj Gaekwad to communicate with their team," Armaan said, "Their grandfather died a long time back."

"Just to keep up a persona?" Karan frowned. "The question is what is this business where a doctor like Udit could be involved with a person like DK."

There was silence in the room, everyone at a loss for words, while Sharlee continued to hammer the keyboard.

"Sir," Sharlee interjected, "Priya, Udit and DK were together at school right from kindergarten. Like them, DK gave a medical entrance too. But he gave up after he failed twice went into the pharma field instead."

"You have more?"

"Yes, Sir. Based on DK's company's audit reports and the bank transactions that the NCB has unearthed, there are a significant number of financial transactions between the Zenith Hospitals and the Apex School chain, all done through several shell companies. Money bounces all over the world then goes to the school. In addition to that Zenith donates a lot to the NGO that runs the Apex chain of schools, DK is one of the Directors," she finished with a flourish.

"Tushar goes to one of these schools, right?" Armaan asked.

"Yes."

"Hmm… Junaid, after this meeting, I want you to visit both Zenith Hospital and Tushar's school, Apex. Take a feel of the atmosphere and the layout of both the places."

"Yes, Sir."

"Be on guard."

"Yes, Sir."

"Trisha, how did you get acquainted with the Gaekwads?" Rao asked.

"With my brother's special needs and my studies, my father was finding it difficult to make ends meet as a freelance physiotherapist even though he was on the list of various hospitals. One day, he was called to Zenith Hospital and offered a permanent job. I don't have the details of what had transpired but that day, my father was ecstatic when he came home. He was given an unmatched salary package with a team of physiotherapists under him. He said someone had recommended him to Dr. Udit Gaekwad. Needless to say, we all were happy."

"Then?"

"I met Dr. Priya at a hospital event, where my father was invited. It was a family event. She was quite impressed to know that I was studying MBBS. After the party too, she kept asking my father about me and even offered a scholarship if I needed one."

"Did you take any financial help from them?"

"No. After my MBBS I didn't need anything since my MS stipend was more than enough. But after I cleared the next entrance exam, she offered me a job in her chain of hospitals."

"And you joined after completing your degree."

"Yes."

"Why? If I'm right, you had a fellowship offer from AIIMS."

"Yes."

"Why did you then join Zenith hospitals?" he asked when she kept quiet and didn't volunteer further information, "Trisha?"

A sliver of shadow ran into her eyes. She blinked and it was gone, but Rao caught on.

"It's important that you tell us everything if you want an end to this mess, Trisha. They sent someone to kill you. The person who died in your apartment was a killer on hire."

"You will say it's a cock-bull story," she muttered, her eyes downcast.

"Try me."

"What do you know about my family?"

"Your mother died after giving birth to your brother—internal hemorrhage, and your father died in a road accident."

"No. My father didn't die in an accident. He was murdered."

Rao raised his eyebrows. "But the autopsy report says something else."

She took a deep breath. "Yeah, sure, according to the official papers," she made quote marks in the air, "...he died in an accident. What they failed to mention in the report was that both his kidneys were missing."

❦

CHAPTER TWENTY-THREE

For a few seconds, no one in the room spoke.

"How do you know that both his kidneys were missing?" Rao asked.

"The assistant with Dr. Sharma, in charge of the morgue, was Kishore Mishra, my father's best friend," Trisha rubbed her forehead to ward off the fatigue.

"Assistant? Would he know if an organ was missing?"

"Yes. He had been assisting Dr.' Sharma for many years and he knows everything there is about a dead body. Maybe more than the doctors. Dr. Sharma is on their payroll."

"Whose payroll?"

"Gaekwads. But I don't have any proof."

"Why would anyone take both the kidneys?"

"There is an illegal organ transplant racket going on at Zenith hospitals." There it's done. She had finally revealed what she had kept to herself for so many years. And it was such a relief.

"Racket? Why would they do that? Donors are everywhere."

"What's happening are not some ordinary transplants. The patients' medical parameters like blood group, DNA and others are closely matched, more than normal, with that of the donors, then the transplants are conducted. These patients are not listed in any of the government-approved list, waiting for the donors. These exclusive, niche operations are being done for select patients who can afford the cost, with a seventy-five percent success rate. This kind of rate is unheard of. The surprising fact is not the surgery or the success rate itself, but that if an organ is rejected, they are able to source another within days."

"How did you come by this information?"

"My father and brother have a rare blood group, the Bombay blood group—rH negative." She sighed. Saying out loud what she suspected, no, what she knew, for such a long time, was definitely a relief. Sharing the information with who she knew were the right people, who could do something about it, took a huge load off her chest.

"So, you think they were interested in your father's organs—and could be interested in your brother's organs—because of their rare blood group?"

She took another long breath and began. "I don't think. I know. While they are performing these surgeries, some four or five in a year, for patients who come through word-of-mouth, I think there is someone sick, someone close to Priya and Udit, whom they are treating, whose kidneys have failed and they had used my father's. And my brother is being kept close as a backup."

"Sharlee, I want the Gaekwads' family tree and details of any surgery anyone in that family has had in the past ten years."

"On it."

"So, you began suspecting them based on what Mishra saw during your father's postmortem. Why didn't you approach the police for another postmortem?"

"He told me after my father was cremated."

"Why?"

Trisha remained silent pinching her finger, staring at the table.

Rao's eyes narrowed. "Are you shielding him, Trisha? Was he part of their team?"

"Yes." Trisha closed her eyes. "He couldn't live with it. My father was his friend," she whispered, "since then he has dedicated himself to us."

"Junaid, I want Kishore Mishra brought into the holding cell."

"Yes, Sir."

"Please, don't do this." She raised her eyes to the screen at Rao.

"He is a potential witness, Trisha. His testimony will be crucial if we are able to unearth anything and if the case goes to court. And he'll be safe with us."

She sighed and rubbed her eyes again.

"Why didn't you leave Delhi?"

She smiled. "I did. I studied really hard for my postgraduation entrance and made sure I could get admission in any college I wanted, away from them. But got the surprise of my life when Dr. Priya visited me at my college in Bengaluru. That was the day five years back I knew I couldn't outrun them. I had to confront them."

The room was so silent that one would hear if a pin dropped.

Trisha continued, "I don't have any proof for my father's murder. The only thing I know is that this all started ten years back when my father was employed with her. We were so happy that our fortune has changed. What we didn't know was that she was planning to steal his kidney because of his blood group for someone."

"Who could that be?"

"I don't know. So far, whatever I have got from the patients' records there hasn't been a kidney transplant for somebody with the Bombay blood group. I have looked at almost all the patients' records since my father died which are public. Either his kidneys were taken to a different hospital or the corresponding records are kept somewhere else. Dr. Priya has patients coming in from abroad too."

"As far as I know, one kidney is enough. Then why both?"

"Even after the surgery's success rate, an organ's life is limited. They took my father's kidney twice." A sob hitched in her throat, but she composed herself and continued, "They took one kidney in the garb of removing his gall bladder. The second time, he was thrown in front of a running vehicle to make it look like an accident." A tear fell down her cheek, but she seemed to be focused on something on the table, oblivious of everyone in the room.

"If you think they were keeping Tushar close, it must be for someone close to them. Did you try to find the blood group of all the Gaekwad family members?"

Trisha's eyes misted again. "Yes, I have blood records for all the members from three generations of their family. But no one has the Bombay blood group." She looked at the tissue in her hand as if surprised it was there, then wiped her eyes. "When Kishore Dada told me about my father, he also warned me that they are dangerous people and that I should not do anything in the heat of the moment."

"Did you find any of the donor records?"

"No. So I began to dig deeper. And got to know that they are performing many illegal organ transplants, niche and for rich. All hush, hush. There are three to four minimal staff members who are always present during these surgeries. No other person is allowed to get involved."

"What kind of records do you have?"

"I have patient records for most of the organ transplants that have been done at the hospital since the time I joined… Every record has a donor and a receiver code, which is the norm to maintain privacy on both sides."

"Why didn't you approach the police?"

"Didn't know whom to trust. Almost all the politicians, celebrities, come to Zenith. I have seen the Gaekwads hobnobbing with the most powerful people in the country. Moreover, I have the records of the organ transplant patients, but I don't have records of the corresponding donors. And I have never seen a donor walking in or a fresh dead body brought in for which we have the consent." She took a deep breath. "The question is from where are the organs coming. Where are the consents? I think those are kept somewhere else."

"So where do you think they could have kept the donor records? Are they really important?"

"Yes, of course. There could be any number of complications, during and after the surgery. We need the history. For such cases, the records are kept indefinitely."

"So where could the records be?" Rao looked at the ceiling.

"Maybe there is another hospital where the donors come and the organs are donated."

"Where are the surgeries happening?"

"I think on the top floor of the hospital. Both the top floors at the hospital and at their Lutyens bungalow are off-limits to people. While I understand privacy at home, but, at the hospital, that floor is like a five-star hotel, and I have never seen anything worthwhile happening there. And yes, they have helipads at both locations. In the back garden of their residence and on the roof of the hospital."

Pride surged in Armaan's chest at the thoroughness of the information she was giving. She had researched them well. She could have made an excellent agent if they had had her in their organization.

"And where is this data that you have collected?" Karan interrupted.

"One copy is on my laptop, which is missing, and one is in the main hospital building. There is a room that houses the supplies—medical supplies. I have taped the pen drive to the base of a cupboard there."

"Please say, you have another pen drive too?" Karan looked at Trisha, his eyes shining.

She looked at Karan. "Yes, Karan, I have a second backup too."

⸺⸺

DAY 18, EVENING
SAFE HOUSE, NEW DELHI

The sun was setting deep on the horizon. Trisha had given them everything. Now it was up to them. They had taken a break for lunch to give Sharlee, Junaid, and Armaan some time to gather data. They all had some decent e-skills and worked diligently on whatever Sharlee assigned them.

While Karan went out again to bring Tushar's toy truck in which she had hidden the second pen drive. Sharlee arranged a laptop for Trisha so that she could help too in whatever small way possible, which meant she had to study cryptography so that she could decipher the code of the patients who had had an organ transplant when the list would be available to them.

After studying cryptography science for two hours, she went upstairs to check on Tushar who had gone to sleep after lunch. Trisha had had a difficult time with him. Woken up in the middle of the night, as well as alert due to the new surroundings, he had been cranky. Thankfully, he hadn't stirred and was sound asleep.

Trisha closed the bedroom door and turned to go down and found Armaan coming up on the stairs. He moved to his right and she moved to her left at the same time. He shifted to his left and she mirrored him. He expelled an exasperated breath.

She stood biting her lip as he looked on, his face unreadable—his whole stance unapproachable.

All of a sudden, he took hold of her shoulders, pinned her to the wall, and placed his lips on her. The next minute, she was kissing him back. Every rational thought went out of her mind as her arms went around his neck and she pulled him closer.

She could taste rum on him. Rum? Was he not on duty? Was he allowed to drink while working? Her fingers slid through his thick hair and his ran on her waist, and her misgivings about rum and duty went flying out of her mind. There was nothing left except the heat, the friction of his hand on her skin, and boy… she remembered… the man could kiss.

Her heart was thudding and lust running through her veins. Her hand was on his neck and the other spanned his wide, sinewy shoulder—nice, she remembered—then she slid her hand under his shirt.

From down below, came the sound of Sharlee cursing the computer and Trisha pushed him like hot coals. He lifted his head and looked at her without leaving her. When she began to squirm under his smoldering gaze and dropped her eyes to his neck, he left her and went to his room.

She stood there wondering about what had just happened.

⎯⎯◈⎯⎯

DAY 18. EVENING
IGI AIRPORT. NEW DELHI

It was time to leave this life behind, DK thought.

It was time to disappear as he had planned so many times. As it was both his children were studying abroad and his wife was visiting them. He could also go out of the country, but it meant never meeting them, which was fine. He had some money stashed abroad and it would be okay if he lived there, free of family shenanigans. It would be a fresh start.

Yes, it was time to leave this life behind.

After an hour in the bathroom, he looked at his reflection in the mirror over the sink. A new face looked back at him—the skin was a bit darker, eyes brown-green instead of black, and beard gone. He picked up the wig and put it over his gel-slicked hair. He had already worn the ill-fitting, slightly worn clothes he had in his goto bag. Putting on the horn-rimmed glasses, he looked like an old professor and the photo that was in the passport he'd be using now.

Picking up a small briefcase that had a couple of medical journals, he opened the front door of the small room he rented. Locking the door behind he hailed a taxi.

The wig was starting to get itchy by the time he reached the airport. After clearing the security, he went straight to the washroom. A janitor was standing in a far corner mopping the floor.

Barring the first stall, all were unoccupied, but he went to the last one. He opened the door and heard footsteps shuffle behind him. Before he could turn, someone put a hand over his mouth and twisted his neck in one swift motion, arranged him on the toilet seat, and closed the stall.

The man then picked up the mopping paraphernalia and left the washroom.

⸻ ❖ ⸻

CHAPTER TWENTY-FOUR

"So, if Udit and DK are together, and Udit is performing the surgeries, what is DK's role in this?" Karan began when they met again in the evening.

"Supplying donors," Armaan replied.

Sharlee gasped, staring at the monitor she had been frantically working on.

"Yes, Sharlee," Rao asked.

"There have been multiple personal transactions through banks abroad between Gaekwad and DK, again buried under lots of false documentation and coming through various bogus accounts. Dr. Priya Gaekwad has been a Chief Guest at the school twice since the school opened fifteen years ago."

"And."

"The woman, Nalini Iyer, who is the Chairman of the Board of Directors for the school is a good friend of Dr. Priya. They have even taken several holidays together."

"Sharlee, look at Iyer's and DK's family tree too. Check if there's someone belonging to the Bombay blood group, and if someone needed an organ transplant or had a deadly disease and died untimely. Go back at least three generations, that ought to cover it. What do you have on the Gaekwads?"

"Gaekwad's father was a doctor too, as was their grandfather. Both men died quite early. The father died after a prolong kidney problem—he was on regular dialysis for almost ten years—and the grandfather died due to liver failure."

"There you have the organ failure connection. So who else in the family is sick now and in need of an organ transplant or has had an organ transplant?"

"That's what is frustrating. I have looked at almost all their close relatives and friends and everyone is hale and hearty."

"Sir, all the answers lie in the school or the hospital. We should interrogate the Gaekwads and search both the school and the hospitals?"

"You guys have to give me something solid to ask for search warrants for the Gaekwads' premises, Armaan."

Everyone fell silent.

"Okay, keep digging on the family, their cousins, their friends, from the health angle. Dismissed."

⸎

"Let's look at the drive," Sharlee said.

It was easier said than done. The pen drive was in the battery compartment of Tushar's old toy-truck. Even after a bribe of a tub of chocolate ice cream, Tushar refused to part with his truck, even though he had never played with it in the last one year.

Trisha was able to retrieve the pen drive only after she allowed him to play with his handheld video game console.

"Come on, let's see what's the fuss all about." Sharlee sat in front of a mean-looking computer and rolled her shoulders. As the documents opened, the data on the patients rolled one by one. Every detail of each patient was recorded with the patients' name, then the code name of the donor and their relevant medical details. Every transplant was given a percentage of receiver-donor vital parameters match, which again was above ninety for most combinations. Not every transplant ended successfully but they had a success rate of almost 80%.

"Did you find anything?" Armaan asked when he was back from the HQ two hours later.

"Yeah." Sharlee sighed and rubbed her eyes. "As Trisha said, all we need is the names of the donors against their code and their addresses."

"Okay," Armaan smiled. "You are tired. I'll take over the security monitoring. Go and take a few hours' rest and come back with fresh pair of eyes and mind."

"I guess you are right." Sharlee picked up her communication devices and her water bottle. "It doesn't need any active monitoring. The alarm will sound if the parameter is breached. And this time I have added something so that no one can disable or jam."

"You are awesome," Armaan said.

"You bet."

"If you want, you can lie down in my bed, Sharlee," Trisha offered.

"No, that's okay. I have done this with them quite a number of times. I'll be comfortable." Sharlee went out.

Armaan looked at Trisha. "You okay?"

"Yeah."

"That was very brave what you have done, unearthing so many things about the Gaekwads." He sat down on the chair Sharlee had vacated, near Trisha.

Too close for comfort. "Did you have rum in the afternoon?" she blurted the question she had been dying to ask since he had kissed her on the stairs.

He laughed softly. "Of all the questions you had to ask that one! Tell me something," he pulled her chair toward his and kept an arm over the back of her chair. "Do you really think that night was an error in judgment?"

It was her turn to smile.

"Don't laugh, okay."

"You are like a bee in the bonnet about that night."

"Rejection hurts," he said solemnly.

"Oh Armaan, I didn't reject you. I was ashamed of the way I behaved that night. It was totally reckless and irresponsible."

"I loved your reckless and irresponsible behavior. Would like to repeat it again." His eyes turned smokily sexy, as he leaned forward and nuzzled her cheek.

She blushed immediately.

"And I love the way your face turns pink." His breath fanned her lips.

"Didi!" Tushar called out from the living room.

They sprang apart.

"God! Does he have some advanced instinct about you getting pally with someone or is it something to do with me?" Armaan raked his hand through his hair.

Trisha chuckled. "He gets a little flustered in new surroundings and with new people."

"A little?" Armaan rolled his eyes.

"Didi!" Tushar called out again, louder this time.

"You can tell him he has nothing to be afraid of as far as I am concerned."

A laugh escaped Trisha, "Armaan, he is like a seven-year-old boy, slightly clingy because of the events happening around him. Once he settles in a routine, he will adjust… to you."

"Well, hope so. Listen—"

"Someone please call Tushar's didi!" This time it was Karan. "Else there'll be a tsunami in the living room."

Laughing out loud, Trisha ran out of the room.

DAY 18. MID-NIGHT
SAFE HOUSE. NEW DELHI

After the first bout of sleep for almost four hours, Trisha was wide awake and alert. It was that moment in the darkness when everything seemed surreal and the future looked bleak as if she was trapped in a nightmare.

She glanced at Tushar sleeping next to her and her heart settled a bit. It wasn't a nightmare anymore. Her brother was safe and united with her, with the best IB team guarding them. The whole week now could be termed as a bad dream, but not a nightmare definitely. And the man she loved—

She sat up straight. Where did that come from? Had she ever thought about loving someone? Never. Then now? Had she fallen for him? No. Yes. No, no, it couldn't happen. It wasn't practical. And what about him? Was he looking for a long-term relationship?

A little agitated, a little restless, Trisha got up from the bed and stood at the window. She hadn't had a rosy childhood and considered herself a realist. How could she think of falling in love with someone she has known for just days? That too under such bizarre circumstances? She stood contemplating her future but couldn't see any clear path. The full moon out in the sky too did not lend any peace to her mind.

Probably a cup of cold milk would soothe and lull her into sleep. She went downstairs and stopped short at the last step. The person plaguing her heart and mind was sprawled on the reclining chair, probably sleeping… or not. Now that she knew him a little she couldn't be sure.

He looked peaceful though, unlike the waking hours when he was on constant alert, and appeared to be always observing, thinking. It was a treat to watch him without a care. He was quite good-looking—when he was not scowling, she concluded—sharp features with high cheekbones and a chiseled jaw. Feelings tugged at her heart again, as she fought the urge to touch his long eyelashes, which could make any girl envious.

"What are you looking at?" he suddenly spoke without opening his eyes, making her gasp.

"Oh, god! How do you always know?" She was barefoot and had been very quiet while coming down the stairs.

He opened his eyes. "Were you admiring me again?"

"I… er… Yes." She had to go from there, else she would end up embarrassing herself. Sensing her thoughts, his hand shot out and caught her wrist, and pulled. She stumbled and fell on him.

"You can admire me all you want. I don't mind."

Acutely conscious of every contact point, right from her hip on his thigh to her hands braced on his chest, she felt his heartbeat in a steady rhythm against her hand. It seemed it was only her heart that was in turmoil. He seemed to be the least disturbed with her presence.

"I think we should make the most of the time while your brother is not guarding your virtue." He traced her hairline and tucked a lock of her hair behind her ear, then leaned in to kiss her cheek. "Else we both will stay overwhelmed with the hormones, electrons, and neurons flowing between us."

"Overwhelmed? Neurons? What are you saying? Someone will come!"

"Don't worry. Sharlee is sleeping upstairs and Karan is in the monitoring room. He dare not interrupt us."

"Oh." She tried to get up but he didn't let her move, tightening his arms.

"Stay. It's relaxing." He shifted a bit and pulled her beside him so that they were now lying toe to toe and hip to hip. He ran his finger over her jaw, caressing her cheek and lips, touching the bruises gently. "I don't like these marks on your face."

"They'll fade away. I'm not in pain." She slipped her hand beneath his shirt caressing his chest. "Sharlee was telling me you always go for the toughest and longest assignments."

"You girls managed to gossip between the briefing and debriefings?"

"Yeah… I was curious about you and since you are not willing to talk, I asked her when she was setting the computer for me in the conference room," she said. "You were with them for more than two years. Two years without any break, living like a drug addict with them in the slums." She shuddered.

"Oh, it was nothing, my cover was very good and the information that I was getting wouldn't have been possible if I would have come back just because it was too long."

"I must have been real bad."

He sighed. "Let's pretend we are starting afresh. Forget everything in between."

"Okay," she whispered, feeling his need to create some good, relaxing memories.

His hand framed her face, and his thumb caressed her skin underneath. Angling his head his gaze dipped to her lips. He waited for a breath as if asking for her permission.

Steadying her heart, she lifted her chin.

Something triggered in him when she offered her lips to him. This was what he had wanted. This was what he needed. All his life. Holding her face, he flipped her back onto the couch and planted his lips on hers. Trisha sighed as if she had been waiting for that contact for a lifetime. Time stopped turning.

There was no need for a talk.

⸻⬩❖⬩⸻

DAY 19, MORNING
SAFE HOUSE, NEW DELHI

"No touching my sista, Amaan!" Tushar snapped at Armaan, the moment he entered the living room with a mug of coffee in the morning.

Armaan sputtered struggling not to spit his coffee all around, while Karan sniggered.

"Tsk…tsk… You better be discreet, brother, or sweeten the kid, before…you know…" Karan chuckled shaking his head.

Mortified, Trisha kept her gaze on Tushar's drawing book that he had left in the living room last night. When did he spy on them? Thankfully Sharlee was still upstairs.

Karan was on a roll. "Nope, I'm not going to intervene. He is the head of the family and has to look after the family honor." Karan grinned. "Me, I have no such issues. I'm totally cool if Trisha compromises your honor. Take permission, man. If not, be discreet."

"Wha is the meanin of disceet?" Tushar demanded from Karan.

"Er… I think you will have to refer a dictionary. I'm a little busy," Karan said and went into the control room.

Trisha couldn't help but laugh but bit her lip when she saw Tushar glaring at Armaan, rotating the pencil in his hand.

Armaan glared back at him, then went into the kitchen. Again.

***

A few minutes later, Trisha gasped when she saw her brother's drawing book. "Tushar, what have you done to your drawing book?"

"Wha?"

"Why have you ruined these drawings?" She held the book toward him. "Why have you smudged these figures, that too so callously with a black crayon?"

He put his chin on his chest and stared down.

"Tush, what happened? Are you upset? Sorry, I shouted at you, but why did you do this? Who are they?"

"My friends," he whispered.

"What? Speak up, Tush."

"My friends."

"Are they not your friends anymore?"

"No."

"Why? Did you have a fight?"

"They are dead or lost."

"Dead? Lost? What are you saying? So many gone!" She flicked the pages, one after the other and it suddenly struck. "Oh my God!" She looked up and found both Armaan and Karan staring at them from across the kitchen counter. The drawing book fell out of her hands.

"Fucking hell!" Karan said.

"No swearin," Tushar interjected.

"Hush." Trisha kept a finger to her mouth.

Karan paced the living room, pulling at his hair as if he hadn't heard them. "They are using innocent people, students, inmates of the special needs school who might not even have a family to protect them, for their nefarious means. And if they are orphans no need to even take consent."

"Or if the inmates had a family, they would invent fake reasons that they died of natural causes or some vague illness since they are unable to explain their problems properly. No wonder the receiver-donor match had such a high percentage and no dearth of donors," Trisha said, "we have to get the medical records of all the students admitted and taken out of the schools somehow if we have to establish the link."

"And if they are orphans and have died, where are they taking the bodies for cremation or burial?"

"The schools are the key. How many are there in the chain? A charitable school. No one questions. No one will question if everything is running smoothly."

"Didi, upset."

"No, I'm not upset with you Tush. Complete your homework, then we'll have cookies and milk."

"This is big and horrendous. From the drug mafia run by that DK to Nayak to Gaekwad and now this!" Sharlee said.

CHAPTER TWENTY-FIVE

"They have just vanished into thin air! My men aren't able to pick up any chatter about her anywhere, neither in the Intelligence Bureau nor in the police." Udit Gaekwad paced the length of his home office. "Sister, a bloody pain in the ass."

"We never included her in anything. What could she have known?" Dr. Priya asked wringing her hands.

"She may have some suspicions about the transplants."

"You think she guessed something was amiss about her father?" Priya watched him with troubled eyes twisting and ruining the silk scarf in her hands.

"Yeah."

She sighed. "I have often wondered about her when she came back after I met her back in Bengaluru. I thought she guessed something was wrong so left Delhi, but she came back again and I was happy. Do you think we should remove Surya from the premises?"

"No. I want you to distance yourself from all this, Priya."

"No way!" She stood up, her eyes now moist. "Can't leave you. I can't live without you."

"You have to be strong, darling. If need be, I'll take all the blame, then you can be there to take care of Surya."

"No way—" Tears came into her eyes. "Why is this happening? I don't want anything to touch Surya or us. It's mother…"

"No."

"She had cursed me." She turned away, arms across her stomach, bent as if in pain. "She never understood us and blamed me that I've led you astray. The woman is always to be blamed, she said."

"She was wrong. Forget the past, Priya." He shook her shoulders.

"We killed her, Udit. That's the reason Surya is suffering and we are suffering."

"Keep quiet. There is no point in rehashing the past."

"I remember her eyes when she woke up when we were giving her the injection that caused the cardiac arrest."

"I said, keep quiet!" He took her in his arms and rubbed her back. "We had no choice. You have to be strong. For him. Pull yourself together. You can do it. I want someone to be there for him, for a long time. And you are that person, Priya. One of us has to be with him."

"Yes."

⊱✦⊰

DAY 19. AFTERNOON
SAFE HOUSE. NEW DELHI

Trisha came up to fetch something from her room. Armaan came in and closed the door and pulled her into his arms.

With a surprised squeal, she too wound her arms around his neck and buried her face in his neck.

"God, I'm so scared of your brother."

Trisha smiled. "He just needs time."

"Yeah, I know. Do I really need to take his blessings?"

"What do you think?" she asked smiling into his chest.

"I guess I have to."

"Then you'll have to."

Someone knocked on the room. "Didi, my crayon broke."

Armaan rolled his eyes. "I'm telling you he has an antenna at the prospect of sharing you with me," he whispered. "I'm dead sure."

She chuckled and freed herself of his embrace and ran to the door. "Coming, Tush," she said and closed the door after her.

⸻

DAY 19, AFTERNOON
APEX SCHOOL, NEW DELHI

"Why do I have to always play nursemaid to him?" Junaid complained, as he drove the silver Mercedes toward the special needs school, spiffy in the crisp blue driver cum guard's uniform.

"It's my innate charm that gets me the better role." Karan, on the back seat fiddled with his tie and wriggled his toes. The black, formal shoes were a bit tight for him, but he had to make do for the meeting today.

"Cut down the chatter, boys," Sharlee's voice came over the speakers, loud and clear.

"Hey, you are not supposed to call us boys," Karan muttered.

"If we are boys, you are in the crib, Sharlee," Junaid said.

"She's eyeing your job, boss." The chatter died down after Sharlee's muffled squeak, then the embarrassed chuckle, as Karan addressed Rao.

There was a radio silence once the car stopped in front of the gate of the Apex School. Karan was meeting Nalini Iyer posing as a rich businessman, K. Jammwal, pretending to be a rich businessman with a special needs younger brother.

They identified themselves at the guardhouse and were waved onwards after the identity check. Nalini Iyer was personally standing at the reception since Sharlee, posing as Mr. Jammwal's personal assistant, had hinted at a huge donation that might be forthcoming if Mr. Jammwal was impressed with the facilities at the school.

"Mr. Jammwal." She folded her hands.

Karan too reciprocated her greeting. "Mrs. Iyer."

"I am so happy that you have shown interest in our school."

"Have heard some very good things about your school. Looking forward to seeing the premises. More so the hostels since he will stay here. I'd like him to have all kinds of comfort. Don't worry about the money."

"Yes, of course."

"If you don't mind can I bring my bodyguard along too? I don't go anywhere without him."

Mrs. Iyer glanced fleetingly at Junaid and said, "Yes, of course."

While Mrs. Iyer took Karan and Junaid around. The cameras on Junaid's cap, hidden by the metal emblem and uniform buttons captured the various entry and exits points, and the positions of the security cameras inside the premises. By the end of the tour, they had a fairly good idea about the security setup in the school and its weaknesses.

Assessing the security detail at Zenith Hospital took them only two hours since Trisha had given them quite a good description of the layout and the hospital was open for public 24X7.

⇒•≻+◈+≺•⇐

DAY 20. EARLY MORNING
LUTYENS. NEW DELHI

The Gaekwads' Lutyens bungalow had state of the art security. The maintenance hub that took care of the central AC, the elevators, and the other electrical consoles was situated in one corner of the premises near the boundary wall.

This arrangement gave Junaid and Karan the best opportunity to get data on the layout of the premises and the security setup. The fact that most of the camera feed was on Wi-Fi and was being relayed on three phone devices, Priya's, Udit's and Susan's, made it easier for Sharlee to hack.

At precisely three a.m. in the morning, a van stopped on the road opposite the rear boundary wall of the Gaekwad residence. Sitting at the back with Junaid and Karan, Sharlee had done her homework and tapped the keyboard of her laptop, "Residence camera feed tapped. Recording." After ten minutes, she said, "Real-time camera feed replaced with the loop recording. Karan, you are good to go."

Carrying his guitar case, Karan jumped out of the back door and jogged to the tree across the boundary wall. He climbed the tree and found a good branch to sit on. He balanced the case on his lap and took out the parts of the sniper rifle. After putting together the rifle, he balanced the empty case between two branches. He screwed on the silencer and looked through the viewfinder. He could clearly cover the whole house or anyone approaching the maintenance room near the boundary who could be a threat. Angling his head toward his collar button, he said clearly, "I'm in position."

A motorcycle slipped into the shadows near the wall and stopped just near the corner. The three of them heard Armaan. "I'm in position." He was stationed as a backup if anyone spotted Junaid on the road, while Karan watched for any security guards inside the premises.

Sharlee said, "Perimeter security alarm jammed."

Junaid hefted his maintenance bag and got down from the van. Walking casually, he reached the boundary wall of the bungalow, threw the bag across the wall, and in one jump was inside the premises. "I'm in," said Junaid.

Three minutes later, he was out the same way and back in the van. Armaan went back the moment Junaid was secure inside the van. Karan dismantled the rifle and climbed down and entered the van, then they headed back home.

⟞⟞◈◈⟜⟜

DAY 20, MORNING
LUTYENS, NEW DELHI

The next day at 9:15 a.m. when both the doctor twins were at the hospital. The temperature controller of the central AC stopped working at their residence. The regular maintenance guy was called but he couldn't solve the problem since the temperature sensor behaved erratically because of the device Junaid had planted near the compressor, out of sight.

The call to the company that had installed the central AC, was rerouted by Sharlee's to her phone. She took the complaint and assured the housekeeper that someone from the company would visit them in half an hour. Junaid, posing as the company staff, reached the bungalow wheeling in a heavy bag, half an hour later.

"What's in this?" the guard asked.

"My tools," Junaid answered.

"Such a big bag?"

"I may not need it though. Let me check the outdoor unit first. If required I will wheel it to the maintenance room. For the time being, shall I leave it here?"

"Yeah, sure."

He left the bag in the foyer and accompanied the guard to the service room. He glanced back, there was no one in the foyer near the bag. He clicked a buzzer. The bag slowly opened from inside. Karan came out of the bag and closing the bag raced up the stairs.

Junaid fiddled with the AC unit in the maintenance room till he got a signal from Karan that he had finished filming the locks on the upper floor. Junaid then removed the device, from the space he had inserted it near the temperature sensor, and closed the unit. He asked the guard to switch on the lever on the panel and the central AC hummed into operation.

Junaid calmly came out of the premises wheeling the case. He stowed the case into the back of the van and drove off.

DAY 20. EVENING
SAFE HOUSE. NEW DELHI

"We know the entire security setup of the school, hospital, and home," Sharlee said as everyone logged into the video conference in the evening.

"Sir, we can go into the school and their residence to search for the donors' records, now that we have a way to get in without any hitch," Karan said.

Rao's phone rang interrupting the meet.

"Rao… yes… yes." Rao then put the phone on the speakers.

"What is the Intelligence Bureau doing with a crime inside the country?" A man's voice boomed in the room. "Do you even have an idea of the ripples caused if you interfere in Gaekwads business? Release Dr. Trisha Mehra immediately and stop poking your nose in the Gaekwads financials." The line went dead.

"Team, that was the CJI, warning us to mind our own business."

"His son was admitted to the Zenith hospital last year," Sharlee supplied the information.

"What was the ailment?"

"Liver transplant."

"Okay, let's do it, boys. We have only this night before the cavalry will descend and take the decision away from us."

⸺⸺

DAY 20, EVENING/ NIGHT
SAFE HOUSE, NEW DELHI

They all huddled in the control room with Rao on video conference. "We will go to the Apex school and their bungalow after midnight. Remember, however, that we don't have the warrants. So, it should be a quick in, snoop, and out. There will be three main teams. Karan and Junaid will go to the school. As per Junaid's surveillance report, there is nothing in the buildings where day scholars have their regular classes. The most likely places where the donor records could be hidden are the hostel, the mess, or the places that are inaccessible to general students or inmates, like an office or a safe. In addition to the records, we are looking for a cremation or a burial place. Junaid, care to elaborate?"

Sharlee displayed the map of the school on the screen.

"There are only two hostels and one office for the hostel warden," Junaid said, pointing the cursor at the relevant buildings. "Behind the mess, there are two rooms, a storeroom and one more room that is always locked. There is a kitchen garden behind the mess which is not open to anyone but the warden and the head cook. Those are the places we are suspecting. Security is minimal. No camera, no electronic alarms. Sir."

"Okay," Rao took the baton again, "The second team will go to the Gaekwads' residence. The surveillance report tells us that, though the building has three floors, they use only two, ground and first. The third floor is sealed. No lights have been seen and no movement from outside. Even their regular domestic staff doesn't go on the third floor. Armaan will handle that part of the operation with Balwant and Trisha."

He lifted a finger when Armaan glared and opened his mouth to protest.

"Sharlee will be in the e-surveillance van near the house. I have men watching all the key members of their family and their security personnel. We have their phones tapped and will know any movement or conversation. I'll be in the control room and connected with all the teams. Remember, we have to gather just the evidence. Any unfriendlies approach, you are not to engage, just abort. Any questions?"

After a couple of routine questions, Rao said, "Sharlee, here, has a new gadget to open the electronic locks."

"Yes, Sir." Sharlee picked up a black palmed size console that had a number keypad and a small display that could show only one line of text. "Most of the new security locks are either opened with a swipe card or password. If their lock needs a password, you just need to fix this on the password keying-in panel of the door. The device will read the last password and display it on the screen here." She tapped the panel above the keypad. "And if the lock requires a card swipe, you need to insert this card."

She picked up an ordinary looking card that had a flat, small chord, about 8 inches long dangling from it. At the end of the chord was a USB socket. "And fix it to the same device here." She tapped the small socket on the edge. "This programs the card to open the door. Got it? Here you go." She handed one each to Junaid and Armaan. "If for some reason, the locks don't open, just give me a signal. I can read the data from the same device on my console, and I will try to open the locks from my laptop remotely."

"Everyone get ready with your bulletproof gear. Remember to keep your communication channel open but the chatter minimum." Junaid was spearheading the entire operation in the field.

Armaan paced the small control room in their safe house muttering something under his breath.

"Everything is going to be fine, don't worry," Sharlee said as she picked up her laptop. "The Gaekwad house is at minimal risk. We have ample security here."

He glared at her then went up to Trisha's room, where she was watching Tushar who was sleeping. She looked at him and came out closing the door softly behind her. "I don't think he will wake up during the night."

"Did you speak to Rao? You are not coming to the operation."

"No, I want to do this, Armaan. I want to know what is that need that drove them to kill my father and threaten my brother. Please. I'll not be a burden on you."

He pursed his lips staring at her for a few seconds, then said, "Don't take any ID or personal items with you. Wear snug clothes and boots. Sharlee must have arranged them for you."

⸻ ❖ ⸻

CHAPTER TWENTY-SIX

Trisha and Armaan reached the Gaekwads' residence a few minutes after two a.m.

"E-security around the parameter disabled, phone network jammed at the residence," Sharlee's voice came loud and clear in their ears.

The silence of the darkness could have woken the dead. Trisha thought that her heart would come out of her chest when they approached the back boundary wall. Balwant went across the boundary first, then Armaan gave her a leg up and she was on the other side in no time. She was not as graceful as Armaan, who also followed her in the next minute, but nothing mattered as she was one more step closer to the truth she had been seeking for so many years.

"We're in," Armaan whispered.

With steady steps, he walked beside her to the rear portico door, his confidence rubbing off on her. He had the device in his hand that he fitted over the e-lock and the door opened with a soft click. He pushed the door and they stepped into the back room, which was a family living room. The stairs from here went up to the second floor. They put on their night goggles as it was pitch dark inside. Trisha remembered the placement of the furniture from her previous couple of visits and led Armaan directly to the circular wrought iron staircase that took them to the second floor.

Just a few minutes behind Trisha and Armaan, Karan and Junaid left their four-wheeler at the end of the lane, ready in a position to flee as soon as required. "We are outside the school," Karan reported.

"E-security of the parameter disabled, phone networks jammed at the school," Sharlee said, over the communication network.

Scaling the boundary wall of the school didn't pose a problem. They were inside the premises within seconds. "We're in," Junaid said.

The three-story-high building blocks stood in eerie attention. Everything looked sinister in the half-moonlight and yellow high-mast lights placed strategically around the two parallel blocks. Taking the cover of the buildings, Karan and Junaid moved toward the mess and the storeroom behind one of the hostel wings, another three-story, box-over-box kind of red brick building.

They kept reporting their findings as they cleared the rooms behind the mess. They could find nothing in the mess, in the kitchen or in the storeroom. Karan entered the warden's room and kept the cotton wad soaked in chloroform on his mouth. After making sure he would be no threat, they began to search the room.

⚬•≼◈⊪≽•⚬

Another electronic lock secured the main door that would give them access to the second floor. Armaan fixed the device again on the lock, but nothing happened. He frowned, looked at Trisha, and tried again, but the screen remained blank.

"Sharlee, the device is not working on this lock," Armaan muttered into his collar.

"Oh, keep the device fixed over the lock. Let me try from here."

Minutes ticked and Trisha felt sweat gathering on her nape. What if they were not able to open this door? What if someone came?

Suddenly, there was a loud click, and Sharlee said, "Got it!"

Armaan went low and Balwant high with guns in their hands, silently scanning the space and found themselves in a small living room. There was an open kitchenette in a corner and two doors on their right. The floor had blue lights, like those in the planes to guide the passengers when the cabin lights were dimmed.

"Shit," they heard Sharlee exclaim softly.

"What happened?" Armaan froze lifting a fist up, a signal for Trisha and Balwant to stop.

"They have an infra-red, movement-based alarm. This one has triggered an alert somewhere inside the house. Abort. Now!"

"Okay. Keep calm. We'll be out in two minutes," Armaan said.

"All clear. It's a bathroom," Balwant called out from Trisha's right.

"This one seems like a studio apartment," Armaan said softly from the door at the back.

There was a double-door in front. Taking a deep breath, she pushed open the door. Soft, muted night lights, recessed low in the walls all around, welcomed them into what looked like another living area with a full-length glass window on the left front wall. It had to be a one-way glass since nothing was visible when they were outside.

They took off their night goggles and let it hang around their neck. The garden below was lit with soft, garden lights and was in full bloom. It was a beautiful sight.

The wall in front had a state-of-the-art entertainment center complete with a 3D TV, video games console, home theatre. A few board games and a Rubik's cube were kept on the coffee table in front of the sofa. Here too there were two doors to the right. Everything was pleasant and friendly.

Trisha went to the first one and Armaan to the second, while Balwant stood alert at the threshold of two living areas. Armaan raised a finger and opened his door, then shook his head. "No one around."

Trisha opened hers. To her surprise, a small boy, around ten years of age, sat on a study table, writing in what looked like a diary. The pallor and his body structure told her that he was critically ill and perhaps, recovering. He sensed them a second later.

"Hi," he said and gave them a feeble, tentative smile.

"Hi," Trisha said.

"Are you my new staff?"

"No. What do you need a staff for?"

"I'm not well. I have Solar Urticaria and another problem."

"Oh."

"It's a bit complicated," he remarked when Trisha picked up the charts and reports from a plastic envelope attached to the bed.

"Don't worry. I'm a doctor." To her surprise, he was almost fourteen. As she read the reports and his vitals, and saw Bombay blood group rH negative, her eyes filled up.

"And you." His eyes shifted to Armaan. "You don't look like a doctor."

"No, I'm not."

"Where is your mother, Surya?" Trisha asked.

"She thought I am sleeping, so she has gone to sleep too." A naughty smile played on his lips.

Trisha too smiled at the little one and scanned the comfortable room, suitable for a child his age. "Are these your parents?" She pointed to a picture kept on the side table of the bed, where the boy was flanked by Priya and Udit.

"Yes," the boy replied.

⎯⎯⎯◇◆◇⎯⎯⎯

DAY 20, MID-NIGHT
APEX SCHOOL, NEW DELHI

Junaid patted the walls for any hidden recesses and hit the motherlode behind one of the *almirahs*. They opened the *almirah* and traced their finger along the shelves. Finally, he found a loose wooden panel under a shelf. Hidden beneath the panel was a lever, which when turned, opened a door from where they could see the safe with an e-lock.

"Bingo." Karan clicked his fingers.

"Wait!" Sharlee instructed, "there might be an alarm here too like the one at the residence."

Karan heard buttons clicking in his earpiece before he heard Sharlee's voice again. "Okay, now put the device."

It took thrice the time it normally took to open the lock but open it did and Karan heard a faint 'yesss' from Sharlee. He didn't have time to think why she was so excited, because inside the safe were numerous hard disks, pen drives, and files.

They quickly packed the entire lot in the two bags they had brought. Closing the safe and replacing the panel, Karan and Junaid went out as they had come in without disturbing anything.

Only the warden would wake up in the morning with a headache, maybe.

———❖———

DAY 20, MID-NIGHT
LUTYENS, NEW DELHI

How dare you!" The voice behind them had Armaan pivoting with his gun aimed at the woman at the doorway beyond the room. It was a second elevator apparently not in the floor plan of the house.

The boy gasped. "Oh, don't hurt my mamma!"

"No one's getting hurt if everyone stays where they are," Armaan said.

"Ma'am?" Trisha automatically addressed her as she had always done. "We don't mean any harm. We just want to know what's going on?"

"Just want to know, huh?" Dr. Priya chuckled, moving toward the boy. "Just want to know?" She shook her head. "It is nothing but survival."

"Survival of the richest?" Trish quipped.

"Survival of the people who deserve this world!"

"Oh, really?"

"You may think whatever you like."

Trisha stared at the woman. "Did my father die for…?" She spread her hand toward the bed, unwilling to blame the child.

Priya stood stoically and didn't answer.

"And my brother is to be another sacrificial lamb? Again for your own?"

"You can't prove anything."

"No one should think they are God. Why did you do it? What were you thinking?"

"If your brother would have had such a problem, wouldn't you go to any length to save him?"

"No."

"Ha!" Priya chuckled. "Easier to say."

"No, it's not. There are so many people suffering. Have they resorted to killing someone to give life to their own? My father died and your… lives."

"You don't know what a mother can do for her child."

"Oh, I know, even though I may not have given birth to him. I've raised him like my own. I know the feeling very well." Trisha blinked back her tears. "You then went on to build on this idea? Was my father your first victim? Did that give you this idea?"

Dr. Priya laughed out loud. "What will you do if you get an answer?"

Trisha's hand fisted.

"I'm so disappointed, Trisha. Given your intelligence, I thought you would have some interest in the greater good. I wanted you on my team. The inner circle, but you could never gain my trust with your snooping all around." She tapped the table, rattling the medicine bottles on it.

"At what cost?"

"There is always a cost. For everything."

"What have you paid?" Trisha asked between clenched teeth and she instinctively stepped in front of Armaan, as another door opened which she thought was the washroom and someone fall behind them.

"No one moves," Udit appeared at the doorway with a gun trained at Trisha.

From the corner of her eye, she saw Balwant slump on the floor and another man step over him with the gun pulled at Armaan. Oh God, did they kill Balwant?

"Put the gun down, Gaekwad. You have nowhere to go," Armaan said with his gun on Udit, recognizing DK's bodyguard Jadhav behind them. It meant that either DK had fled or was dead.

"No," Udit said.

"What's the point? You have just killed an IB agent."

"He is not dead," Jadhav said.

"You will have to surrender anyway. We have the evidence and the witnesses." Armaan heard Karan whisper in his ear that they were going to surround the Gaekwad residence. *'ETA, ten minutes,'* Karan updated him.

"You are bluffing." Udit smirked.

"We found everything at the school—"

Priya gasped and clutched the boy.

Ignoring her, and happy to see a sliver of fear in Udit's eyes, Armaan continued, "—and this conversation is being recorded, Gaekwad. You of all people should know how we operate."

"And now we have everything covered," Udit said, as his aide Marathe came inside and put the gun on Trisha's temple. "We will have her as a hostage and you will let us go."

"Daddy, don't do it," the boy said.

"Don't worry, Surya. Priya move."

Priya picked up a bag from the credenza, took the boy's hand, and pulled him back toward the elevator she had come in.

On the other side, Marathe prodded Trisha to move to the other elevator near the stairs, through which they had come up.

Udit's eyes never wavered from Armaan. "My helicopter is landing in the garden as we speak. I don't want anyone approaching us, and interfering, or she dies." He backed a step covering Priya and his son.

"Do you think we care if a civilian dies?" Armaan smirked, though his mind was half numb since the time he had heard the click of the safety catch of the gun trained at Trisha's head.

Udit laughed. "This will not work Major Armaan Joshi. As you said we know how you operate and also who is your weakness."

'All the elevators, jammed.' Armaan heard Sharlee's voice in his ears.

"What's wrong, why is it not responding?" Priya jabbed at the button panel inside the elevator cabin.

"This must be his doing," Udit shouted and aimed the gun at Armaan.

Then everything happened simultaneously!

From the corner of his eye, Armaan saw Balwant stir and aim the gun at Jadhav. He pivoted, covering Trisha from Gaekwads, and took the shot at Marathe's hand, as Balwant neutralized Jadhav.

Marathe grunted and the gun fell down his hand. Trisha gasped when she saw Armaan jerk and someone moving in the kitchenette. Instinctively, she stepped on her left to cover Armaan and heard the shots.

A searing pain on her left arm, had her rooted to the spot. She thought she heard another shot before sinking into blessed unconsciousness.

⊸⧫⧫⊸

CHAPTER TWENTY-SEVEN

Trisha came around at the hospital to find Armaan sprawled on the easy chair to her right, his eyes closed. And Tushar was sitting on a stool on her left with his head on the bed, clutching her hand. She didn't know whether Armaan was asleep or was in his thinking mode, but Tushar was asleep because his face was turned on her side and he was drooling with his mouth open.

She caressed his hair lightly so as to not disturb him. But he did get disturbed, wrinkled his nose and turned his face to the other side, and continued to sleep. She glanced up to find Armaan watching her.

"You were shot!"

"Udits's doing, but I was wearing the bullet-proof vest, remember. All said and done, he is not street smart. I would have aimed at the neck. That's the most vulnerable part."

"Don't, please. I've had enough. How did it go in the end, though?"

"We got them, and everyone. Once Marathe fell, they had no choice but to give up. At one point, I felt Udit will shoot himself, but then he looked at Priya and the boy, and surrendered."

"And at the school?"

"We have all the records of the lost students, and residents. Their cremation records too."

"Oh, my God!"

"They had a CNG cremation facility. It's a nightmare for the families and the survivors."

"Oh." Her eyes welled up.

"Except a couple of the old staff and Ms. Paul, who had an apartment at both the hospital and their home, none of the household staff was allowed on the upper floors. The kid hasn't met anyone in his life except his parents and staff."

"How was she able to hide the pregnancy? His birth?"

"Apparently, she told everyone that she was going on a trip abroad, but was in India at Ms. Paul's village."

"What about the kid, Surya? His life will change. Why do people develop such abnormal attachment? What drives them toward such an unhealthy relationship?"

"God only knows! Somewhere, something is deeply wrong in their psyche. It's a bit creepy and a bit disgusting, besmirching such a pure, sweet relationship."

"Yeah. Probably their ego and superiority complex makes them believe that no one else matches up to their expectations. What will happen to the child?"

"He will be well looked after, Trisha. He has family money. I guess a trust will be established so that he is never in want of money."

"Hmm… it must be so devastating for him. No wonder he had so many health issues."

"You have such a high compassion quotient." He kissed her temple. "By the way, you weren't supposed to jump in front of me like that, I was wearing a bloody bullet-proof vest."

"Even I was wearing one." She chuckled. "It was reflex. I didn't think." She glanced at her bandaged shoulder. "It's a flesh wound, they told me."

"Thanks for saving my life," he said softly.

"It was due. You have been saving me all this while. Who pulled the trigger on me?"

"Ms. Paul."

"Oh, the Dragon." She laughed out softly.

"What?" He caressed her hand running his thumb over her skin.

"The warden at Zenith. Ever since the time Gaekwads invited me to their home, she has been very jealous of me. Not that she had any romantic feelings toward Udit, but she didn't want anyone close to them except her. Was someone else injured?"

"Yes. I shot her too."

Trisha let out a soft laugh.

"She just barged in and pulled the trigger. She'll live." Armaan looked at her and took a deep breath. "So. Am I allowed to kiss you or will I have to take his permission?" Armaan glanced at Tushar still sleeping face down on her bed.

"You can kiss me now and take his permission later when he wakes up." She smiled as she caressed her brother's hair.

Armaan leaned in and rested his head on hers as he muttered. "You gave me such a fright, going limp in seconds."

She traced a finger along his jawline. "I'm here. I'm okay"

"I was so, so angry with you for not confiding in me. Wanted to just dump you there at the farmhouse… your supposed aunt's home… Do you know all along the way I kept thinking about ways to impress your aunt so she'd invite me to stay over with you?!" He chuckled before getting emotional again. "I felt like a fool seeing the gun in your hand trained at me."

"I'm so sorry."

"Wanted to leave you there… but couldn't. I couldn't leave you there." He sighed caressing her cheek. "So many bruises, so much blood spilled."

She looked at him. "It's okay. It's over," she said again. She knew about his parents and the trauma both the brothers had gone through. Sharlee had told her.

"You have to know, there is nothing that I won't do for you."

Her eyes filled up. She wanted to hug him hard and never let go.

"Don't cry, okay? It hurts. As does looking at the bruises on your face and the worry and fear in your eyes."

She tried very hard to control, but a tear still rolled down her cheek.

"Trisha, please."

Since she was not in a position to think anymore, she settled for something mundane to distract herself. "I was admiring your eyelashes. Do you have any idea what girls do to get eyelashes like yours?"

He scowled. "You are saying I have eyelashes like girls?"

"Umm…"

"No way."

"Come closer."

He smiled and sat down on the bed and kissed her eyes, cheeks. By the time he came to her lips, she took over and bit him on his dimple.

"That was sneaky…" he said enduring her assault silently.

"I have been dying to do this since that night at the Oberoi when I noticed your dimple."

"No talk of dying, getting injured, or driving for a long, long time. I can already hear my knees trembling with fright."

"Okay." She chuckled.

"Don't kiss my sista, Amaan," Tushar growled sleepily, rubbing his eyes and getting up.

Armaan lifted his head and looked at Tushar. "Easy now. I can't help it, buddy, you better get used to me."

"Cos?" He scowled at the two of them.

"Cos, we are together."

"You are?" Tushar's eyes narrowed. "Like girlfriend boyfriend?"

"Yeah. Aren't we, Trisha?"

Tushar looked at Trisha, who dared to nod and smile a bit. That made Tushar consider the fact, and he nodded. "Okay. Then, it's okay."

Armaan let out a soft laugh and went over to hug him.

EPILOGUE

The door opened and they came in like whirlwind.

"We bought almost the whole store!" Tushar dumped the grocery bag on the kitchen counter.

"Did you?" Trisha looked at him and Armaan and smiled. It felt her chest would explode with happiness. Karan and she were cooking dinner. Tushar and Armaan had brought the dessert, which meant all kinds of ice creams and cakes. Armaan was unable to say no to Tushar, indulging and spoiling him.

"Yeah, the man at the store said so and was very happy."

"I bet."

"Hey." Armaan bent forward and placed a kiss on her temple, then began to stack the ice cream in her refrigerator.

It had been two weeks since she had been discharged from the hospital, and Armaan and Karan had been busy with winding up the case, completing the paperwork. She had planned to quit Zenith and join another hospital. This Saturday they all were together for the first time for a meal. Armaan and she had decided to spend the rest of his holiday together.

"We are going to complete our game," Tushar declared, "Come on, Amaan."

"Sure, but wash your hands first," Trisha said.

"Trish, where is the red chili powder?" Karan called from the kitchen wearing his handkerchief around his head like a chef's cap and her strawberry patterned apron.

She handed him a fresh packet of chili powder. "You think this is required?" She asked leaning forward to peek into the pot. Karan was cooking pot roast for the past two hours. She has her doubts about what he was doing because he was randomly sprinkling the spices he found in her kitchen.

"Yes, of course." Karan added a pinch of chili powder then tasted the curry again and added coriander leaves a third time.

"Yesss." Tushar shouted from the living room. It seemed the scrabble game with Armaan had resumed.

She sighed. In any case, if Karan's dish didn't come out well, she had enough chicken-biryani for the four of them.

"Cooking is like developing a relationship."

"Really?" She gave final touches to the greek salad she had been preparing, adding a few mint leaves to the bowl and hoped the brothers liked the dishes she had prepared. Not that she was an expert, but she could cook a few things quite well.

"One should take it slow and gauge the emotions. Sometimes you know, in the heat of the moment..." he adjusted the flame of the stove, "...one feels something but with the passage of time it fizzles out."

"You think so?" She frowned. A seed of doubt sank into her mind.

"Yup. Never ever go into it with emotions so high that when they drop, things don't seem as great as they do."

"Oh?" she answered on auto, picked up the salad bowl and placed it on the credenza instead of the dining table, and sat down on the dining chair with a thump.

Armaan took one look at her and shouted. "Karan what nonsense are you spouting!"

"I am saying what the experts say."

"What is this word? I don't know this word," Tushar said.

"One minute, Tushar." Armaan got up.

Wasn't it the same? Trisha thought nibbling her lower lip. They have been thrown into an unusual situation, where she was dependent only on him, and he had to save her because he was wired that way. Shouldn't they take it slow?

"My mother used to say patience is the key to a delicious dish," Karan continued unmindful of the turmoil in her mind.

"Uh…hh…" Trisha nodded. What if Amraan's love for her fizzled out in a month or so? Under normal routine, what if he began to feel the burden of having Tushar with them? What if he resented the whole situation after some time and would be too polite to say so?

"Trisha, are you all right?" Armaan panicked when he noticed her pinching her fingers. All the thoughts, of a sexy night with her when he would peel off her denim shorts and white lace-top, went out of the window. The distant expression on her face meant sheer disaster!

"Yeah, of course." Her head bobbed as she took a deep breath.

"I think we need to talk." He stood before her. "Come on, get up."

She looked up at him and bit her lip. "Armaan, I—"

"Amaan!" Tushar called.

"Just a minute, Tushar."

"My pot roast is ready, tan-da-daa." Karan came to the living room holding the pot with gloves and placed it carefully in the middle of the dining table. "Trisha, why did you place the salad there, bring it here fast. I'm starving." Karan took off the gloves and rubbed his hands together.

"Karan, you are a complete ass… idiot."

"No swearin," Tushar interjected now looking at the adults curiously.

"What did I do?"

"To make amends please complete the game with Tushar. Trisha, come with me," Armaan said and pulled her up.

"Armaan," Trisha couldn't utter anything other than his name.

"Don't freak out, Trisha! Just give me a minute." Armaan glared at Karan.

"But what did I do." Karan took off his handkerchief cap then peeled off the apron.

"Armaan, I think we should—" She came out of the trance when he pushed her into her bedroom and closed the door.

"Don't say anything right now."

"Though inadvertently, Karan has raised an important point. We should take a break from each other, say for, at least six months."

"He was talking about cooking, Trisha."

"Yes, but it's a valid point… we did meet under bizarre circumstances and we—"

"We met under extremely simple and normal circumstances at the party. And—"

"That was just lust."

"Talk about yourself, baby. I totally knew you are the one for me." He pulled her into his arms.

"You are just making that up."

"No. I met you at the party, then at the mall parking, then on the highway, two days at Ambala." he ticked off the days on his hand. "That's a span of eleven days. Eleven normal days. I knew you were the one. Am absolutely sure…"

"But Armaan—"

He pinned her to the wall. "If you are having doubts about your feelings—"

"No, I—"

"Then it's settled, we are going steady. No talk of living apart for six months." He placed his lips on her.

"Oh, Armaan, don't do it. I can't think." She breathed in and nuzzled his cheek. Her hand automatically went to his chest, then around his neck.

"Then don't think. Thinking is totally overrated," he whispered against her soft skin.

"What are they doing? I'm hungry." Armaan heard Tushar say, then Karan answered.

"Tushar, have you ever had hors d'oeuvres?"

"What's an hour de vruh?"

"Something to be had before the dinner."

"Is it?"

"Yes. Do you want to have one right now?"

"I'll ask didi."

"No, no. We are friends. No need to ask didi. Come let's go."

Silence reigned in the living room after the main door clicked shut.

Slipping his hands under Trisha's top, Armaan smiled against her lips and thought Karan had redeemed himself adequately.

*** END***

Do you think Karan deserves story of his own? Well, most of the readers seems to think so. So on popular demand the next one coming under 'Undercover series' features Karan and Anamika. Write to me and suggest a name for the book.

AND

Read the others books in Undercover Series if not read already, 'The Bodyguard', or 'Guardian Angel'.

Though connected in sprint of love and loyalty they all are standalone stories.

Acknowledgements

Sometimes words are not enough, but still, they need to be said. Thanks a lot, Leena, for reading my terrible draft and giving me insight into the story, which otherwise wouldn't have occurred to me. You made my work shine.

Thank you, Neelesh for reading a genre that is not one of your favorites, and if you are reading this ack, you know the book is published, so you can gift it to whosoever you want to.

Thank you Nikita Soni for all the help and understanding a writer's dilemma. You are the best.

Thank you, my editors, for accommodating my changing deadlines. This one was really tough. You guys are awesome!

Last but not least, thank you, my family members, and my Isht for every support visible or invisible.

RUCHI SINGH
THE BODYGUARD
UNDERCOVER BOOK #1

GUARDIAN
Angel
UNDERCOVER BOOK #2
RUCHI SINGH

RUCHI SINGH
BLOOD
TRAIL
UNDERCOVER BOOK #3

Author's Note

Thank you for reading 'Blood Trail'. I hope you enjoyed the story as I relished writing it particularly Trisha's character, who had endured so much in such a short span. She had taken such a huge responsibility in life that she deserved Armaan and all his love and support!

The next in line is Karan's adventure. I think after helping Nikhil and Armaan find their life partner, he deserves his own story.

Word of mouth is an author's best friend and much appreciated. If you enjoyed, please consider telling your friends and/or posting a short review on Amazon and Goodreads.

Thank you,

Ruchi Singh.

www.ruchisingh.com

Email: author.ruchisingh@gmail.com

Amazon: Author Page

Instagram: @ruchiwriter

Twitter: @ruchiwriter

Facebook: Author Page